# What R
*Fin*

"Life has its ups and downs. We wonder why things happen the way they do. Janie Upchurch resonates hope and insight through the eyes of a young girl as she journeys through a life filled with great difficulties and joyous triumphs. God's timeless truths prevail."

Kay Dokkestul —
Missionary

"This book is so heartwarming that I often found myself with a smile on my face as I read through the pages detailing Elizabeth's captivating journey into adulthood. Elizabeth shows wisdom beyond her years thanks to the importance of her personal relationship with the Lord and the practical life lessons imparted by her lively grandmother. There is tenderness and charm among the pages of this book, and I thoroughly enjoyed taking the journey with Elizabeth and her remarkable family and friends."

Ellen Crider —
Research Attorney turned
Stay-at-Home Mom

"*Finding Herself Blessed* is a must read, especially for women who need encouragement in the face of difficult life circumstances. The heroine, Elizabeth, relies upon her exemplary faith in God and adherence to strong moral principles and life lessons that have been laid before her by a father taken from her early in life, a loyal, Godly grandmother, and ultimately the love of her life. Janie has written in a masterful way that will enable you to relate to the heroine and be strengthened and encouraged by her life choices. The book is most inspiring, even for a guy!"

Gary Williams —  
Associate Vice President for  
University Relations/  
Alumni Services, Union University

"*Finding Herself Blessed* by Janie Upchurch is a heart warming story about God's amazing love and grace! Make sure you are in your cozy reading place....once you start you won't want to put it down until you are finished!"

Sandy Carver —  
Employee Relations Manager  
St. Rita's Medical Center

"I love that God is enough in every circumstance."

Ann West —  
Avid Reader

"Wow, and wow again. How will I ever put into words what my spirit is feeling? To read of the tender care Elizabeth receives from those around her speaks volumes of the tenderness which the Lord desires to impart to us, His children. I feel as though I have just received a great big hug from the Lord! This story has so much potential in women's ministries across the country. It could be a devotional, or an outline for a mentoring program similar to Titus 2. If nothing else, the stories contained herein will serve many a Christian woman as they navigate through the difficulties that life tosses their way, the only way we should-with Scripture and the aid of Godly women."

Peggy Summy —  
Homeschooling Mom

# Finding Herself Blessed

By

Janie Upchurch

*To Ashli ~*

*In Finding Herself Blessed, you will become friends with Elizabeth, her lively grandmother, and her delightful friends.*

*Enjoy travelling with Elizabeth on her walk of faith in the Risen Lord.*

*Much Love!*

*Janie Upchurch*

*Phil. 4:8*

Copyright © 2010 by Janie Upchurch

All rights reserved. No part of this book may be used, reproduced, stored in a retrieval system, or transmitted in any form whatsoever — including electronic, photocopy, recording — without prior written permission from the author, except in the case of brief quotations embodied in critical articles or reviews.

All Scripture quotations, unless otherwise indicated, are taken from the *King James Version*. Copyright © 1982 by Thomas Nelson, Inc. Used by permission. All rights reserved.

FIRST EDITION

ISBN 9780981935669

Library of Congress Control Number:   2009935681

Published by
NewBookPublishing.com, a division of Reliance Media, Inc.
2395 Apopka Blvd., #200, Apopka, FL 32703
NewBookPublishing.com

Printed in the United States of America

# Dedication

I dedicate this book to my husband, Eddie, who has encouraged me ardently, assisted me logistically, and courted my dream with me. When I asked him what he thought his role in this book has been, he jokingly said that he was the model for the hero of the story. He has indeed been my hero in this captivating adventure.

# Acknowledgements

Thanking:

My husband, Eddie, whose patience was immense concerning my computer ignorance and whose constant encouragement through the times that I was thwarted, helped me to make it to the finish line.

My daughter, Emily, who followed this story from its rough draft on, reading it more than once in its unfinished form and addressing chronological details as well as kindly pointing out things that I had not made clear to the reader.

The many family members and friends who encouraged me to pursue my dream of writing a book.

Nanorimo, for being the impetus for my writing a novel as my first book.

My mentors and encouragers at Reliance Media:
Jen McGuffin Smothers, who directed me to Reliance Media. Patrick McGuffin, owner of Reliance Media, who excitedly

opened the door to publishing possibilities for me.

Angela Shaw, who walked me through every step of preparing for and publishing this book, teaching me much along the way.

Derry Sampey, my editor, who is a renewed acquaintance from my distant past, and who periodically became my right arm. Or is it my write arm?

My Mac "one to one" instructors, Stephanie and Adam, who directed me in formatting my manuscript for submission while also showing genuine interest in the book's progress.

My neighbors and friends, Katy and Neil, who graciously allowed me to use their house on the book's cover.

# Elizabeth's Favorite Scripture Verses

*Proverbs 31:26* "She openeth her mouth with wisdom; and in her tongue is the law of kindness."

*Galatians 2:20* "I am crucified with Christ: nevertheless I live; yet not I, but Christ liveth in me: and the life which I now live in the flesh I live by the faith of the Son of God, who loved me, and gave himself for me."

*Ephesians 4:32* "And be ye kind one to another, tenderhearted, forgiving one another, even as God for Christ sake hath forgiven you."

*Philippians 1:6* "Being confident of this very thing, that he which hath begun a good work in you will perform it until the day of Jesus Christ:"

*Colossians 2:6-7* "As you have therefore received Christ Jesus the Lord, so walk ye in him: Rooted and built up in him, and stablished in the faith, as ye have been taught, abounding therein with thanksgiving."

# Chapter 1

Although Sam was saved by grace through faith in the risen Lord Jesus Christ as a boy, he is drifting from the Lord by the time he finishes high school and joins the Marines in the 1960s. As a result, he is going astray in a Marine base town in southern California, making the rounds of bars and picking up different women every night. Then he meets Rosa. They are both nineteen when she becomes pregnant and they marry.

Rosa's pregnancy is troublesome from the beginning, but they think it is just an extreme case of normal morning sickness, because they know others who have gone through similar, though less severe, experiences. When Elizabeth arrives two months early, experiencing serious breathing difficulties from underdeveloped lungs, she is moved to a critical care ward in a private hospital across town before Rosa can be discharged to accompany her. Rosa has not yet experienced the feel of motherhood, has not even held her baby at her breast, and she is stricken with an acute anxiety that reshapes itself into a prolonged bout of despair, foreshadowing the angst that will characterize much of her adult life.

Fortunately, Elizabeth thrives, and by her first birthday, there are no indications that she will experience lingering problems from her traumatic start in life. But Rosa continues to feel troublesome pangs of self-reproach and doubt. She often wonders if her uneasiness is due to the fear she experienced during Elizabeth's birth and infancy, to her own doubts about motherhood, or to other unsettling events which occurred earlier in her life. So, while she and Sam take delight in Elizabeth and she makes her life appear smooth on the surface, Rosa's private insecurities range from simple distractions to weighty disturbances in her always-anxious mind.

Sam's years as a Marine pass quickly, and just before he is discharged, he and Rosa make the decision to move to New York, where she has a brother. Upon their arrival, Sam joins a construction union and begins working with Rosa's brother, Joe. The pay is good, but the corruption he encounters is bad, a word that also aptly describes the winter weather and the state into which their marriage is rapidly sliding.

Sam would end this progressively unhappy marriage except that he can't stand the thought of losing his little daughter, Elizabeth, who is his heart's delight. It is Sam's sheer dedication to doing his best for her that the Lord uses to draw him into the little chapel, which he passes daily on his way home from the bus stop. Added to that dedication are the fervent prayers of his mother, who aches for her son, his wife, and their baby girl.

Now Sam, who reminds himself in some ways of the prodigal son in Luke, is soft for returning to the Lord of his youth. That prodigal son had a home of great provision. Yet, he wanted to take his portion to do with as he pleased. He squandered it on riotous living. Then he, a Jew, found himself eating with the unclean – the food of pigs in the pen of pigs. He decided to go back to his father and offer to work as a hired servant. Yet his return brought him back to experience once again the full privileges of a son.

Sam is ready to experience once more the fullness of his position in Christ. He understands that his salvation is secure. For a while, he has skated by on that fact, but now is convinced that his lifestyle is a waste, that his marriage is a sham, and that his precious daughter is being brought up as if there were no true and living Lord. It all culminates in the chapel that sunny fall afternoon. He lays himself bare before the Lord, who takes the broken pieces of Sam's life and the brokenness of his heart and sets Sam on a walk with Him that will not waver during those few years that are left for him on this earth.

Later in their small apartment, Sam is rolling on the floor with Elizabeth, both laughing wildly, when Rosa calls them to dinner. Describing it as the most satisfying mealtime in all his marriage would be an understatement, but he is also conflicted. Although he is bursting to tell Rosa of the changes in himself, he fears telling her, because she has so often made it clear that she is not interested in the lifestyle of his mother.

After Elizabeth is sound asleep and the house is quiet, Sam takes Rosa in his arms and kisses her tenderly, saying, "Rosa, today I stopped by that little chapel that we have passed so many times, because I seemed to be drawn inside. It was as if my feet would not let me walk past it."

Rosa's eyes narrow and her teeth clench. She seems to know what is coming. Sam continues speaking in a measured voice as he gently holds her hands in his. "I know it perhaps doesn't seem fair to you to tell you this, since you never knew me as a person who acknowledged my true identity. I am a Christian. I am bought by Christ's blood. I belong to him. I am safe and secure in Him. I am going to live with Him for eternity. Out of gratitude for who He is to me and what He has done for me, I am now committed to living for Him."

Rosa stiffens and pulls her hands away.

Sam is compelled to comfort her, so he says, "I know that you never wanted to talk about things of the Lord except to ridicule. Rosa, sweetheart, I don't even know if you have a background of knowledge. What do you know? Where do I begin?"

"Sam, I don't understand what you are talking about," Rosa says, "and it scares me to hear you talk about things that were not part of our life together. What will happen to us if you get religious on me?"

"Oh, Rosa, please let me explain that we are born into this world with a sin nature. We grow in our sinful ways. We cannot stop sinning on our own, nor can we cleanse our own sin. We cannot be good enough to go to heaven on our own, and would be sent to the lake of fire for eternity; except that God, in His great love for us, sent His perfect Son, Jesus the Christ, to live a perfect life and die a cruel death that paid the righteous price required for our sins. He was buried and three days later rose again from the grave giving us hope for our own resurrection. He fulfilled all requirements of atonement by the Father to secure eternal life for everyone who simply and by grace through faith accepts this free gift of eternal salvation. You can do this, Rosa. Please meet my Savior and accept His gift of life."

"Sam, this scares me! This is all new to me. I don't get it."

"Rosa, I want to do this for you, but I can't. You have to receive it yourself, personally as your very own, through faith in the risen Lord Jesus."

"I don't know where to get that faith," she whispers.

"Faith comes from the Word of God. Rosa, I am going to pray for you daily, and I will share the Bible with you."

Days pass, then weeks, then years. Sam is content while Rosa is still clinging to tangled trepidation. Sam is patient, but Rosa remains tense and nervous.

Elizabeth celebrates her fourth birthday just before Thanksgiving at a party with lots of children, a few gifts, and Rosa's famous chocolate cake with divinity frosting. It is delightful, until Rosa's brother, Joe, brings out his bottle of whiskey and begins pouring drinks for the adults. Though Joe knows well the changes in Sam, he persists in trying to draw him back to those long past days of drinking heavily together. Sam is continually kind in his refusal of the drink and in his request that it be put away. But Joe's reaction is belligerent. It is a scene that has played itself out so many times lately, but one which Sam has decided would not ever play itself out the same way again.

When the guests are gone, Sam and Rosa talk, and Sam shares with her his longing to move back to Tennessee to be near his family and to provide a calmer life for Elizabeth. He suggests that they visit over the Christmas holidays, during which time he will set up some job interviews and they can look for housing.

At first, Rosa pays close attention to Sam's plans, which already seem too specific to her. Although she also yearns for

Elizabeth to enjoy an uncomplicated childhood and for her own life to become serene away from the harshness of the cold, dark, city life, she does not share Sam's eagerness.

Soon, her mind is working overtime as it jumps between listening to Sam and letting her own thoughts run rampant. She is clearly becoming agitated by the thought of living more than a few days with his family, and she is especially fearful of making her home there. Where will she find a friend like herself? Who will care about her loneliness? Who will be patient with her reticence? She embellishes her fears until they overshadow her reason and she burst into tears. Can she force herself to go?

# Chapter 2

That Christmas in Tennessee is when Elizabeth's significant and detailed memories begin to solidify. As a small child, she can see that living in Tennessee brings welcome relief to her father and even to her mother. To Rosa's surprise, she is happy to be with Sam's family, and she sometimes wishes she could grasp their faith and forget reasoning.

Sam finds a service station job as a mechanic, for which he had been trained and at which he had excelled during his four years in the Marines. He smiles, as he works, remembering the story of his Uncle Buddy, during WWII. Buddy had two older brothers who were serving in the Pacific, where they saw some real action. Buddy, on the other hand, had taken typing in high school and was assigned to a stateside position typing dog tags for the duration of his military service. Sam is glad that he has been prepared for the right job, just as his Uncle Buddy had been so many years before.

Sam enjoys working at the station, and soon buys out the owner who, at age 84, is ready to slow down a bit. Not only does Sam excel as a mechanic and business owner, he is also benevolent with his plentiful earnings. His benevolence is discreet, as he often performs work free for widows, as well as those who are ill or temporarily down and out.

Mrs. Waters is one of those. Today, when she comes in with her three children to get gas for their car, she asks, "Sam, do you know where the boys can get a good used lawn mower? They are needing to make some money to help out the family, and they want to cut grass."

Sam checks with some of his customers in search of old lawnmowers. In less than a week he has collected four, from which he is quick to make two nicely running machines with parts to spare.

When he delivers them to the Waters' house, he finds Mr. Waters sitting on the porch for the first time in nearly a year, since the accident that left him partially paralyzed. He has gradually learned to walk again and feed himself, along with all the other daily chores that turn a person back to physical normalcy, but his emotional recovery has been slower to rebound.

Mr. Waters has been a dutiful father and a diligent husband all in the context of affectionate love, so the long recuperation and months of depression have manifested themselves in two very opposing ways. The family is shocked, as they never expected that their strong man would be weakened in this way. They, on the other hand, were well prepared to function during his recuperation, because of his previous years of leadership. They know what to do, how to do it, and what kind of attitude to have about it.

"Hey, Gary, great to see you! I have these two lawn mowers that your boys were hoping for. Where do you want me to put them?"

With the help of the handrail, Gary slowly makes his way down the steps and takes carefully measured footsteps to the garage. Sam opens the door and wheels the lawnmowers in, setting a full can of gas beside each one, with notes attached explaining that as long as there is a need for the boys to earn money to help the family, the cans will be refilled at no expense.

While Sam pumps gas and repairs vehicles, he sings the Lord's praises with his melodious tenor voice. On a still day, you can hear him from as far as three blocks away. His singing has become as much of an institution in Erwin as the chiming bank clock and the ringing church bells. This town of 7,000 is an idyllic place to live and to rear his precious Elizabeth. Rosa flourishes and delights in the homemaking skills she is perfecting in their small brick bungalow, only two miles outside the city limits. She wants more children, but that is not happening. No doctor can give her a reason. She would have doted on Elizabeth anyway, but with no competition, Elizabeth is the apple of the family's eye.

Sam's mother, whom all the family and friends simply call "Mama," is Elizabeth's best friend and confidant. Mama is also Elizabeth's favorite Bible teacher. As they read the stories of Daniel in the lion's den, Joseph and his coat of many colors, Ruth and Boaz, Jesus multiplying the loaves and fishes, and so many others, they act them out. Once when Mama had just thrown bread (manna) all around the living room and dining room floor for them to pick up, unexpected company arrived; and Mama invited them to pick up their share for the day. Things of the Lord never embarrass Mama. She is never embarrassed by anything good. She simply smiles and does her best to help other people smile.

# Chapter 3

Time glides smoothly by for Elizabeth as she enjoys her picturesque life. This fourth Christmas in Erwin, everyone is at Mama's and the girls are getting ready for the Christmas Eve service at Erwin Chapel, when Mama finds Sam asleep on the couch. He is always the one waiting patiently for the ladies, but this time he is still in his work clothes. She wakes him up and urges him toward the bathroom. Soon, she hears him vomiting, and so does Rosa. They both rush to his rescue. The vomiting and gagging are unrelenting. Rosa and Mama get Sam into the car with a barf bag and cold, wet washcloths to clean and soothe him, as they speed down the highway to the hospital.

Elizabeth runs next door to stay and to attend the service with Mama's best and lifelong friend, Aunt Jan, and her nephew, Phillip, from South Carolina. He and his father are visiting for only a couple of days, and he is excited over this Christmas event. But Elizabeth cannot keep her mind on the wonderful program about Jesus' birth. She can hardly remember her part as a member of the heavenly choir. The hot chocolate, sugar cookies, and candy canes afterward don't have any appeal to her. She can only think of her father. Phillip is more help than anyone, as he had spent a holiday once with his mother in the hospital. He tells Elizabeth how he had cried himself to sleep alone in his room so that he would not cause his father any more pain. Perhaps sharing his experience should prepare her mind for when her father comes home two weeks later and she learns the devastating news that he has been diagnosed with stomach cancer, but it doesn't.

"How did this happen to my father?" Elizabeth asks everyone.

Although he lives for several more months, he never goes back to work or regains much strength. Yet his optimistic outlook and vibrant personality are still Elizabeth's to cling to until he draws his last breath. Sometimes, she leans on his chest, wondering how he can still make his chest rise with her weight on it. She loves to hear his heartbeat, and listens intently to see if it beats in rhythm with hers. She snuggles there daily, comforted by the feel of his arm around her. Often, they laugh together, but sometimes she cries. She cannot help it.

One day, during a time that he perceives as an especially teachable moment, Sam says to her, "Elizabeth, I have shown you how to live the Christian life, and now I will show you how to die without fear because of the hope within me, the hope of glory in Christ Jesus. It is a my gift of perpetual guidance for the time when we are apart."

It is true. Her father is the one who introduced her to the Savior when she was five, and she received Him as her own Savior that very day. She has seen Christ in her father so many times, day after day.

Elizabeth remembers her father's kindness. When people

entered his station in an impatient mood, he simply calmed them down, without buckling under their pressure for him to treat them as though they were more important than someone else. Those very people came to respect her father, and she would often later see them in church. Sometimes, their appearance at church immediately followed an evening delivery, by her father, to their home. Even as a little girl, she can see that he used and still uses every opportunity to tell anyone about the Savior.

The irony is that her mother is still struggling with trying to put the Lord in a box and figure Him out. Mama says that Rosa sometimes seems like King Agrippa in the Bible who told Paul that he was "almost persuaded."

As the months pass and Sam grows weaker and weaker, his two mechanics, Bob and Glenn, continue to run the business. They are trustworthy, and Sam has no qualms about leaving the business in their hands after his death. He has a written agreement concerning how he wants things to progress when he is gone – how he wants his dear Rosa and his precious Elizabeth to be taken care of financially.

There is as much company as Sam can handle, with people constantly calling, bringing food and leaving notes of appreciation. Elizabeth is a proficient reader by now, and she often takes the notes to bed with her and cries herself to sleep reading them.

"Sam," one reads, "How would I ever have kept the baby when Bobby left me and the boys and never came back? Our house was paid for and we had church friends who helped us, but we were in an immediate pinch until I could get over the complicated pregnancy and the more complicated birth. When you sent Esther to my house daily until I could gain strength, you saved my home and family."

Another says, "Sam, that little plot of land that you let me garden on for free those three years that we had my sister's four children as well as our own two, kept us in food. Nell canned and froze food, and we never lacked."

The next letter explains, "Sam, while I was out of work for that long stretch, I once saw a stack of envelopes behind your counter with my name on the top one. I know I was not supposed to be behind your private counter, but I needed a pen and you were outside talking to a customer. It seemed okay to me that I could step back there to get one. Yet it is not okay to invade someone's private space and I am sorry I did. But I am not sorry that I know, personally from your gifts to me, that you are the generous man I have long thought you to be. Also, I know that you want the Lord to get the glory, so I will keep your secret."

For her part, Elizabeth thinks, "Now I have invaded Daddy's private space, too. But I want to know more. I will ask Daddy if I can read them."

When she asks Sam for permission to read his letters, he tells her that if they give her a benevolent heart to serve in the Lord's name, she has permission to read and share them after he is gone, but only if the sharing will bring honor to the Lord.

"After I am gone" is a painful phrase for anyone, but especially for a very privileged little girl, whose father is the reason for so much of her privilege.

She wonders, in her eight-year-old mind, how she will make it without his smiles and encompassing tenderness. She knows she will still have her mother, who delights in her, and Mama, who stimulates her imagination and creativity and guards her spirit like a sentry. But no one person takes the place of another.

Sam is so weak by late October, that the family celebrates Elizabeth's ninth birthday early, in case he does not make it until late November. At Elizabeth's request, they have Sam's favorite yellow cake with light chocolate icing, in hopes that he can enjoy it. He seems to, as he eats almost a whole piece, and that makes Elizabeth happy.

For her birthday, she receives a diary so that she can record her days. Her father always thought she had a cute way of saying things as a very little girl. He now thinks that she has a way with words and an understanding beyond her years. It seems natural that he would think of this gift, and she loves it because he thought of it. She knows her father will still be guiding her with memories that will continually surface, and with his words of wisdom and affection that he has scattered throughout her diary to point her in a certain direction just when she needs it.

Rosa is distraught over knowing she is losing Sam, but not about his eternal future. Although she sees that future for him, she is still trying to figure it out for herself. Oh, why does she not simply believe? Mama prays with and for her daily.

When the time comes for the Lord to take Sam home, it is a beautiful fall day, November 1, 1974. He breathes his last earthly breath just before noon with all his girls surrounding him. It is an ambivalent time of joy for his being face-to-face with the Lord, and sadness for his absence from them. Elizabeth has never felt such pain before. It is, however, a foreshadowing of more pain to come.

After the funeral, Rosa and Elizabeth try to find enough to do to fill the emptiness left by Sam's absence. Though she is still a child, Elizabeth has a far better chance at this than Rosa, as she has the Lord. She also has a full day of school five days a week and church on Sundays. In addition, she has Mama. But Rosa is withdrawing from Mama. It is an intense withdrawal, leading to a broken relationship that threatens to never be mended. Rosa cannot go on, because she has no hope. She is caught in a web of despair and is fixating that despair on Mama. Mama can and does go on, because her hope and her son are in heaven.

# Chapter 4

It is only a few weeks until Rosa, without warning, packs her things and Elizabeth's, and moves them back to Buffalo. Taking a job in a nearby tavern to fill her time, she drowns the demons that haunt her with after hours drinking. Rosa is so distraught that she can hardly function at home, leaving Elizabeth to fend for herself. Rosa's distress is escalated by the fact that she tried to believe when times were good and found it too difficult, so now she no longer tries. She feels she's been cheated out of her husband, and she doesn't understand her mother-in-law who can live a life of normalcy despite her loss.

Even though Rosa drinks up her paycheck, they have enough money to live on because of the money they receive weekly from Sam's business. But, money is not the answer to Elizabeth's longing, which is based on such large and sudden loss. She doesn't have a mother who nurtures her anymore, because Rosa is in need of so much nurturing herself. Elizabeth understands her mother's despair, as well as a nine-year-old can, and tries to view Rosa's needs as greater than her own.

Meanwhile, she continues to feel the recurring pain of

complete rejection by Mama. Every week when the check arrives, Elizabeth goes back to Erwin in her mind, and she hopes for a letter, even a note, but her mother says that there is none. There is not a card for her birthday or for Valentine's Day, not even for Christmas. Mama, once her best friend, has abandoned her. Elizabeth's young mind tries to decipher it all, but the variables are too many and the answers are too few.

"She must be really mad at me to forget me completely. I would not have moved if Mommy had not made me. I wish I could talk to Mama and tell her that. I would beg her to still love me," Elizabeth whispers to herself.

Sometimes, she asks her mother to let her write a letter to Mama, and Rosa does. Although her mother addresses the letter and takes it to the post office, Elizabeth never receives a reply.

As the years pass, Rosa continues to work at the tavern, drinking nightly, while Elizabeth worries about her mother's unhappiness and inability to cope. Elizabeth is thankful, however, that her mother never brings men home the way so many of the women she works with do. Their children tell Elizabeth terrible stories of how the men treat their mothers and them. But Rosa has never gotten over Sam, and will not give anyone else a chance at her heart. Elizabeth knows this, and realizes that is her safety net, separating her fate from the fate of the other girls.

Being an honor student, as well as joining many activities and clubs in order to make friends, helps to keep Elizabeth steady. When she is old enough to go to church with friends, she takes every opportunity. Elizabeth revels in hearing someone explain the Word to her and she grows in a plethora of positive character qualities, but the clouded bitterness proliferates, especially at Christmas, her birthday, and the anniversary of her father's death, which all come within a two month period. At a time when families are gathering for Thanksgiving and Christmas, she is most lonesome and most angry. Occasionally, she thinks back to the holidays in Erwin and aches for them, but they are gone.

The best days of her life are gone, never to return. She doesn't even have a friend that she trusts enough to share the deep recesses of her heart. It is not because she has no trustworthy friends. She does. What she doesn't have is the confidence to trust another person who could, and probably would, let her down simply because of being human. She realizes that her needs, if she ever fully voiced them, would nearly drown her, and perhaps anyone else in the path of the raging waves.

Before Elizabeth finds relief from the ever-pursuing pain she tries to hide, her next tragedy is on the horizon. Rosa's drinking has taken its toll on her body and she is diagnosed with cirrhosis of the liver, causing her numerous stays in the hospital during Elizabeth's second year of college. Eventually, Elizabeth drops her classes during the spring semester to care for her mother full time.

Rosa softens with the disease and with Elizabeth's care. But, for Elizabeth, this new pending loss escalates her locked-up feelings of misguided rejection. She knows that she must keep depending on the Lord for strength or she will unravel.

Paul is an attentive boyfriend who loves Elizabeth, yet he has not tapped into the extreme pain that lingers deep in her mind and obscures her ability to be transparent. Elizabeth begins to wonder how she can give him hope that there is a possible future for the two of them together. She cannot give herself to anyone until she experiences a catharsis that will allow her to heal. Suddenly, she realizes that she is experiencing a block to inner healing that is somewhat like her mother's block in feeling that she has to figure Jesus out before she can accept Him. That realization is eye opening to Elizabeth, and she begins to look at her mother's lost condition in a much more compassionate light.

Since Rosa is now too ill to drink alcohol anymore, she is easier to talk to, the way she was in Elizabeth's perfect childhood days. Her mind is clear and her heart is becoming soft. Elizabeth asks her mother if she would like to hear again how to receive Christ and be on her way to eternity with Him.

Rosa answers, "Yes."

Elizabeth clearly explains to her mother about Jesus' abundant, overwhelming, inexplicable, never-ending, unconditional, perfect love for her. Elizabeth wants her mother to hear as many positive words as she can express about the Lord's love for her. She tells Rosa how Jesus longs for a relationship, and that longing is what sent Him to the cross to atone for sin. Each one is paid for by his innocent blood, which is the only sacrifice to satisfy the Father. His death, His burial, and His resurrection secured salvation for eternity.

Elizabeth explains, "Mommy, all you need to do is accept this payment of Jesus, the Christ, the Risen Lord, on your behalf, taking that free gift as your own by grace through faith."

Rosa whispers, "I understand and I accept Jesus and His gift of eternal life for me." She smiles weakly, but radiantly, as she continues, "I wish Sam were here for this moment."

Elizabeth agrees with her mother that Sam would have loved it, and explains to her that though there is no marriage in heaven, she will still spend eternity not only with the Lord, but also with her beloved Sam.

Elizabeth's heart cannot stop rejoicing as she reads Scripture to her mother several times a day. The pastor comes often and people from the church bring food. The outpouring of concern is an amazing experience for Rosa.

The days pass, sometimes slowly because of the wearing constancy of caring for someone day and night; and sometimes too rapidly as they escalate the arrival of the day that Rosa goes home to heaven and leaves Elizabeth an orphan. Although she is an adult, she will be an orphan just the same.

Before that day arrives, Elizabeth takes over the mail, which is the last job Rosa gives up. Even in the weakness of her final days, Rosa continues to have her friend pick up the mail at the post office and bring it directly to her, then sends her friend back to the post office with the outgoing mail. The mail has been so much her mother's domain that it never, until now, occurred to Elizabeth that she could be part of it.

This time when Rosa's friend brings the mail, Elizabeth explains, "I will be handling everything, including the mail, from now on."

Panic consumes Rosa, and her weak voice pleads for her friend to give the mail to her as usual. With a look of resignation, her friend places it into Elizabeth's hand, turning her head away to avoid eye contact with either of them. First, Elizabeth sees the monthly check from the business and next, she sees a letter addressed to her from her Mama.

"I have not heard from her since I was nine, and I now I am nineteen," Elizabeth thinks. "What is this about? Has she heard about Mommy?"

Elizabeth retreats to her bedroom to open the long-awaited missive in private, trying to quell her mixed emotions. On the one hand, she thinks it's about time. But on the other hand, she thinks it's too late. Still, she begins to read:

"My Dear Elizabeth,

Once more, I am writing in hopes that this letter finds itself in your hands and makes its way to your heart. For the ten years since I last saw you, I have written to you weekly. As each letter is returned unopened, I pray to the Lord to keep you spiritually safe, and to let you know somehow that you have not been abandoned by me.

"Losing Sam to eternity with the Lord was personally difficult, but followed a normal course of the disease. Losing you to the unknown has also been personally difficult, and much more heart wrenching, as I know that you have been purposely kept from my love. Worse still is that a little girl, who has, by the number of years gone by, obviously grown into a young woman who has been left to question one of the fundamental relationships of her life and likely come up with rejection as the answer. If this letter comes back to me, it will be put into the box with all the others in hopes that someday you will contact me."

Composure does not come quickly to Elizabeth. Her resentment and bitter feelings are transferred in an instant from Mama to her mother. But Elizabeth cannot leave it there. In a long moment of reflection, she realizes that she has been loved just as dearly by Mama during all those days of seeming rejection as she was in those happy bygone days. She also realizes that her mother was trying to protect her from the hurt she herself could not bear when she lost Sam.

Elizabeth speaks her feelings, saying, "Mommy must have thought if I stayed connected to Mama, Daddy's death would haunt me the way it has haunted her. But, we are very different, Mommy and I."

Suddenly, those thoughts disappear and all Elizabeth can think about her mother is that Rosa is saved, and if she is taking her last breath this very moment, she is just fine.

In fact, Rosa was taking her last breaths as Elizabeth's mind was scanning the years of pain, confusion, and unhappiness. The Lord used that instant to strengthen Elizabeth beyond human comprehension for the immediate task of going back into her mother's room and finding that, although her body was still warm, her spirit had gone to its real and eternal home.

The next few weeks find Elizabeth going through the motions of clearing up and cleaning up. The pastor's wife steps in to be her mentor as she continues to examine her emotions. Elizabeth knows that the bitterness only took a reprieve during the funeral, and that it has truly not been dealt with. It has not been pulled through that hard section of her heart. Rather, it is entangled by the many roots that have wrapped themselves around things that have nothing to do with the original feelings of rejection and pulled them into the mix. Those insidious roots are choking parts of her testimony and witnessing. Even though Elizabeth is honest, hardworking, and kind, she struggles with this infiltration of bitterness. She is spiritually exhausted.

Elizabeth dwells often on thoughts of her mother and she wonders how a heavenly heart feels when it experiences what it longed for so diligently here on this earth. Relishing those thoughts, she still laments the fact that she never got to talk to her mother about keeping her separated from Mama. Nor did she have the chance to discuss her mother's own estrangement from Mama. But in seeing her mother's immense peace at that very late-in-life salvation, Elizabeth truly believes that Rosa would have taken every step to make amends this side of eternity if the Lord had left her on earth longer. Yet she knows, as she knew ten years ago, that His timing is perfect.

Paul has been attentive and gone far beyond the call of duty during the time of Elizabeth losing her mother. His patience is legend, but now Elizabeth is faced with the growing realization that, although Paul truly loves her, she does not love him the way a marriage requires in order to flourish. She has taken a great deal of his strength and given him very little devotion. Until now, that could have been attributed to her situation, but not any more. She realizes she must release him to be the man he is designed to be for the woman who will love him with her whole heart.

"But what is next for me?" she wonders aloud.

# Chapter 5

By June, all of Elizabeth's loose ends are tied up. The snow and ice are finally gone and the lilacs are blooming, inspiring Elizabeth to think about things new and fresh. She determines that it is time to go home.

"Buffalo was not home for Daddy when he lived here, and it is not home for me," she says to her friends.

Although it has been ten years, Elizabeth can still picture in her mind's eye, Erwin and her little house and the service station. But mostly she can see Mama's house, where the entire family's most exciting times were spent.

A lot changes in ten years and she wonders if she'll recognize the area now, if any of her former school and church friends will still be there, and if they will remember her.

As Elizabeth packs her winter clothes and gathers the few summer clothes she owns, she decides to shop for more when she arrives in Tennessee. Her friend, Joelle, offers to drive down with her and return by plane. But Elizabeth prefers to go alone as she needs the solitude to reflect on the wonderful experiences she had with her mother early on and at the end, and to let them sink deep into her soul for the time when she becomes a mother. She wants them to be an integral part of her heritage. Besides, there is no rush. She can take two weeks if she wishes, or three. She can take as long as necessary to sort out her soul. After all, nobody there knows she is coming. Actually, they don't even know she still exists.

Elizabeth is drawn to the small towns along the route and chooses to stay in some of them for her overnights. Perhaps she feels safer there or perhaps she feels a latent kinship. She enjoys spending two days in the same spot on the weekends so she can attend church. It is fun riding around town and praying about which church to attend, and she is never disappointed. Often, a family who sees that she is alone and has an out-of- state license tag treats her to dinner. She spends her time getting to know them rather than sharing much about herself. It seems that there is going to be much for her to learn about herself before she can share it with someone else.

The Skyline Drive, through the Blue Ridge Mountains in Virginia, is the most relaxing part of Elizabeth's drive. When she stops to absorb its beauty, a fawn comes to her car window, and she extends her hand to touch it before it bounds away. She appreciates that the Lord is giving her beauty and warmth in a variety of ways. He knows exactly what she needs, of course. She sometimes wonders why certain things happened the way they did, realizing at the same time that there are hurts in this life which will not be explained, but will be used to drive her to the Lord, for her best and often her only comfort.

Moving on, she decides to go south to Atlanta and backtrack to Erwin, as she has never been to Atlanta, at least not that she can remember. However, she does not think it is the kind of place that a young woman wanders around on her own, so she chooses to be there on Sunday through Wednesday, in hopes of meeting someone at church who will sightsee with her for a couple of days.

She attends a large, established church in downtown Atlanta that she has heard of before. As she planned, after the early service she finds a young adult Sunday School class where she can make her plea for a tour guide. There, she meets three Emory summer students, two girls and a guy, who say they will be available for the next two days after 11:00. Over lunch together, they make plans.

Elizabeth welcomes the comfort of her motel room and the opportunity to rest from the exhaustion of many days on the road, but she is elated at finding Christians who so readily take her into their lives. She had heard that the South is different in its casual friendliness, and she is beginning to believe it is true.

Monday finds them perusing the shops in Underground Atlanta, and enjoying the Coca-Cola Museum. Trying no less than thirty different Coke flavors from various countries is an adventure. But her caffeine levels cause her to beg for water with her supper at Atlanta's hamburger and hotdog haven, the Varsity, before she and her new friends drive around the nearby campus of Georgia Tech.

While they travel the next day to Stone Mountain, the conversation flows. Although Elizabeth tries to ask most of the questions, she also is required to give some answers. When Bo finds out that she is going to Erwin, Tennessee, he is quick to share that he has been there twice with a college friend. "The first time I went, was when Phil included me in a family reunion, and we stayed at the home of his Aunt Jan. The next time I went, I invited myself to tag along, because the first time was so much fun."

Elizabeth's mind snaps back in time, and she wonders if Aunt Jan could be that same Aunt Jan who cared for her when her father was so suddenly taken to the hospital. Could this Phil be the nephew, Phillip, who sincerely tried to comfort her that night of the Christmas program? She is lost for a moment in wondering.

"Does Phil visits his aunt often?" she asks.

Bo answers, "He does, as they have always had a close relationship. And, since it is only three hours away, it is easy to do."

Elizabeth thinks he absolutely must be the one who was so thoughtful concerning her little-girl fears the night her father was rushed to the hospital. It comforts her to anticipate that at Mama's, she may have a sensitive friend who will occasionally be only a shout away. She dreams of this and other contented scenarios without having any clear direction of what will happen when she arrives at Mama's house.

# Chapter 6

On Wednesday morning, Elizabeth sleeps in, then drives slowly back north to Erwin, stopping for a quiet lunch in a small neighboring town and taking time to pray for calmness in her racing heart. She continues to acknowledge that she does not have a clue what to expect when she arrives. She chooses to believe that Mama is going to accept her with open arms, perhaps even smother her with love.

She wonders aloud, "Am I ready for that? Will she give me time alone with her before I have to meet too many others? Will she feed me too much information too fast? Will she cry and make me sad? Will I cry and make her sad?"

In her mind are many more questions. "Will Mama see enough of my nine-year-old self to recognize me? Will she like me? Will we both be too free or too cautious? Will one be too free and the other too cautious? Will I want to run into her arms? Will I have the courage to run into her arms? Have I functioned as an adult so long that I can't be a bit of the child anymore?"

As the questions tumble over each other, sometimes they do not even make sense to Elizabeth. Her life is turning around almost as fast as it had when she was packed up and taken away from everything and everyone she knew except her mother and the Lord. This time though, no one else is physically in control of her. Emotionally, however, she is not certain who is in control.

She drives around Erwin for more than an hour, which is a long time for a town that has only about 7,000 people, much the same as when she left ten years before. She supposes that means the town is stable, and stable sounds great to her.

During her sightseeing, she purposely drives by the service station that still bears her father's name, Sam's Family Service Station. Although she is not out of gas, she decides to fill up.

"Why not?" she says aloud, "I will be paying myself." Finding that an amusing little thought, she laughs at her humor.

Elizabeth wants to scan the service station, inside and out, and reminisce without anyone knowing who she is. She spent many an hour coloring at a little desk in her father's office, in those long-ago summers, just to be with him. Her mother brought lunches there, so they could spend the noontime together as a family.

It all ended too soon for me, Elizabeth thinks sadly as more vivid memories begin working their way to the surface.

Bob is working at the station and she immediately recognizes him, since he has hardly changed. Of course, he does not recognize Elizabeth, which is her plan. They have a pleasant exchange. As she thanks him for the services, she asks for directions to Cherry Street, and suddenly suspects that makes him a bit suspicious. At this point, she feels she must act rapidly, so she rushes the half-mile to Mama's house. She is glad to see that it looks much the same, except for being painted white with navy blue shutters, as opposed to being pale yellow with white shutters, as she remembered.

After breathing deeply, she slides out of the car. By the time she is on the porch, Mama is opening the door.

Startled, Elizabeth asks herself whether Mama opened the door because she recognized her or because that is what people do in small Southern towns.

There Mama gazes long into Elizabeth's face with an expression of disbelief, and softly says, "Elizabeth," with a recognizable lilt in her voice that makes Elizabeth want to fall into her grandmother's arms.

"Should I? Could I? Why would that be any harder than much of the last ten years of my life?" she silently questions herself, knowing that the answer is encased in that so important word, trust.

Suddenly, she composes herself and says gently, "Yes, I'm Elizabeth," though Mama's greeting had not been a question, but an expression of welcome relief.

Mama's eyes tear and then a flood rushes down her face. Elizabeth sobs, too. She sobs for what they seem to have now, and for what they have missed. Elizabeth finds out later that Mama is crying for those things, too, but being older and wiser, she is mostly crying over what they are going to have, another chance. Mama knows how to build. Nothing is ever too late for her. She is exactly who Elizabeth needs, now that she has no mother and no father. The Lord has brought her here to be restored. Mama understands that the restoration will be slow, and Elizabeth understands it, too.

Elizabeth brings her bags into Mama's home and makes it her own, just the way Mama expects. They are slow to spread the news of Elizabeth's arrival, but in a small town, one does not spread news alone. The phone begins to ring and neighbors come to the porch, being careful to not impose, yet showing transparency in their happiness.

Peach season arrives just as Elizabeth is beginning to feel settled in her familiar new home. Every year, Mama makes peach preserves and pickled peaches from the trees in her fenced orchard out back, and this year it becomes their first project together. As soon as they begin, Elizabeth is struck by the familiar fragrance of the peaches and even by the feel of the knife in her hand as she peels till her fingers cramp.

Mama lets her get a sure footing around the house and around town before sharing the letters with her. She senses Elizabeth's need to unwind before having to emote again and drain herself dry.

Her father was an only child and Elizabeth is an only grandchild, but she has an extended family of great aunts, uncles, and cousins. Therefore, although she is beginning adulthood as an orphan, she is presently part of a large and happy group of people who want to erase the pain from her years of loss. They cannot. Elizabeth learned at a very young age that is something only the Lord can do. But although she learned that fact early, it is not, in her case, accomplished quickly.

In continuing her transition, she and Mama decide to enjoy the freshness of summer. They put up vegetables from the garden and truck patches around town during the day, and at night, they sit on the porch swing being entertained by fireflies and their elusive lights. The hummingbird feeders are filled daily to guarantee a constant show by the kitchen window. Mama and Elizabeth picnic by the stream on Saturdays, inviting anyone who wants to join them. Sundays find them singing in the church choir, and eating Mama's famous fried chicken for dinner.

They decide to wait for the long, cold nights of winter to go into the attic and retrieve the box of letters, thinking they will both be ready by then. Some might think that opening the box would bring immediate trust and healing, but Mama thinks it will bring renewed pain, as well as healing. She thinks, for now, that they will continue developing trust just by spending time together, doing whatever comes next. Elizabeth will find out later that Mama is right, that waiting to open the box is indeed wise.

# Chapter 7

Summer passes quickly, and soon it is time for Elizabeth to think about school again. She finds that she has waited too late to get into a nearby university, but perhaps this is God's way of giving her more time to become acclimated and settled. After all, Elizabeth thinks that she and Mama have saved the box for the long, cozy wintertime, since neither of them knows what it will bring. And what is wrong with one full year away from school to do things that count for a lifetime?

She decides to do house cleaning for several older women in their church, on a volunteer basis, for the fall. This will give her not only Mama's wisdom, but also the wisdom of a diverse group of godly women. She asks her pastor to pick the women who need help, and he does. It is true that they need help, but she feels he is also thinking of what they can give to her, and giving to her turns out to be one of the things each woman does best.

Mrs. Bach keeps Elizabeth busy waxing the same table till she can see her face in it, while she tells Elizabeth of her husband and how he was the leader and protector in their home. After they have developed a comfortable easiness with each other, Mrs. Bach encourages Elizabeth to formulate a list of character qualities to look for in a husband, and prioritize them for herself. The next time they are together, they compare their lists, because Mrs. Bach, who had kept a copy of Elizabeth's list, has also prioritized them for her. Elizabeth obviously makes an A+ as their lists match exactly. She then pronounces Elizabeth ready to have a date, and giggles like a schoolgirl.

With a twinkle in her eye, Elizabeth asks, " When I find Mr. Right, will you consider being my matron of honor?"

Mrs. Carter is Elizabeth's conscience, checking on everything she does and everything she says. She wants to be sure that Elizabeth's protocol is impeccable. She has Elizabeth bring her all thank you notes for perusal before mailing them. Mrs. Carter checks the length of her dresses, and once asks her to get rid of the skirt that comes too high up above her knee when she sits down. Elizabeth is more than glad that hats and gloves are no longer in style, because, whether she liked them or not, she would be wearing them. Elizabeth is the epitome of a lady when Mrs. Carter is finished with her.

Mrs. Sims shows Elizabeth how to be creative. There is no room in her house that she does not use Elizabeth to redecorate. Is it because Elizabeth knows what she is doing? No, it is because Mrs. Sims knows what she is doing, and she teaches Elizabeth along the way. Elizabeth learns floral arranging using every kind of flower in the garden. She learns how to set an exquisite table with the Lenox china and a happy and cheerful one with paper plates. Mrs. Sims has flair, which she knows how to pass on. The exciting part for Elizabeth is that she chooses to pass it on to her.

When Thanksgiving draws near, Elizabeth is ready to bring that creativity to life at Mama's house. After cleaning for a week, they reserve the last two days for cooking before all the family members in town and from miles around begin to stream in. There will be relatives present whom Elizabeth has not seen since she was a little girl, and many she has never seen.

"Oh, the excitement of it all!" Elizabeth declares.

Aunt Jan has her usual house full of company also, including her nephew, Phillip. At the mention of Phillip's name, Elizabeth's mind travels not only to that fateful day that her father was rushed to the hospital, but also to the day in Atlanta when Bo told her he had been to Erwin with his friend, Phil, to visit his Aunt Jan.

Once again, Elizabeth muses aloud, "The loosely veiled mystery will now be solved. Is he indeed the same Phillip, and will we become friends?"

Phillip arrives on Wednesday evening, but life is too busy for Mama and Elizabeth to go over and greet him. She supposes he is still sensitive, as he does not come to see them until after their busy Thanksgiving Day ends, and all their company is gone. Then, on Friday morning, bright and early, the doorbell rings and there he stands in his jeans, flannel shirt, and hiking boots.

He greets Elizabeth cheerfully, then adds, "It's a lovely day for a hike. Will you join me?"

She looks surprised, because, even though she knows who this must be, he has yet to introduce himself. Elizabeth glances toward Mama, who quickly takes over the introductions. Next, she rushes Elizabeth to her room to put on a hiking outfit for the event, which has obviously been planned by Mama and Aunt Jan for weeks.

Phillip and Elizabeth drive out to the Okalatchee River, and follow it for miles before stopping to explore on foot. They skip rocks on the water and criss-cross the stream in shallow areas, hoping all the while that they will not fall in. Aunt Jan has sent a picnic along, and they are very hungry before they find Phillip's "perfect" spot, which he says needs a patch of drying leaves to sit on, as well as a spot of sun shining through the crowded evergreens and bare maples. They must be close enough to the stream to hear the rippling of the water and far enough from the road not to hear the passing cars.

What a Shangri-La, and what a thoughtful man, Elizabeth thinks.

They talk about their first meeting ten years ago, and their uncanny connection through his friend, Bo. They welcome the probability that a friendship is likely to blossom out of it all.

During the weekend, Phillip and Elizabeth talk on the porch swing, sit together during church, and have Sunday dinner with Mama and Aunt Jan.

She writes a thank-you note and passes it by Mrs. Carter first thing on Monday for her approval, wishing she had just once thought to write one to Paul for all his thoughtfulness toward her. Perhaps, she will do that now. In addition, shouldn't she know how he is faring, and shouldn't he know what is happening with her?

# Chapter 8

It is less than a month until Christmas, which will probably be slower for them than Thanksgiving was, as they are invited out, rather than doing the inviting and preparing.

Elizabeth had sent out several applications for college earlier in the fall and is now hearing back. With her excellent grade point average, as well as a full volunteer record from her previous school, it turns out that every school she applied to has accepted her.

She speaks aloud to herself, as is her habit when she has questions that beg for answers, "Where do I want to go? Do I want to be far from home or nearby? Do I need space or closeness? Am I ready for long times away and long rides home, or am I not? I think much of that will be decided by the box which Mama and I are getting down from the attic tonight."

It is their plan not to answer the phone or the doorbell while they huddle by the fire and read. Mama had written to Elizabeth once a week for fifty-two weeks a year, for ten years. In doing the math, the calculation is 520 letters, in addition to cards for special occasions. While they prepare their supper, Mama tells Elizabeth about picking out each card for its specific meaning and nuance.

As she explains to Elizabeth how she felt each time a letter was returned and added to the box, and how she sometimes fingered the others, but never gave herself permission to do more than touch them, Elizabeth realizes that reading the letters will perhaps be as cathartic for Mama as it promises to be for her.

It is plain to see that going through this stack of mail will take much longer than it takes to simply read the words contained in 520 letters. It will take time to let each letter, written to a girl, settle into a woman's heart. It will take time for Elizabeth's mind to span a wide range of feelings that do not come from the letters themselves, but from her years of longing for them, and then realizing they truly did exist during those painful and trying times.

In the end, Elizabeth will see clearly what she already knows as truth, that life is so often not what it seems, and we hurt ourselves immensely, and hurt others, too, by second-guessing and imagining. Still, we are human and it takes much growing in the Lord and diligently practicing His principles to reach abiding wisdom.

They take their soup and crackers into the living room and settle at a table by the fire as they open the perfectly ordered box. Elizabeth did not expect that, in addition to her letters, there would also be letters to her mother. Elizabeth's mind dwells on the fact that Mama never forgot either of them. Even though she knew that Rosa was the one returning the letters, Mama continued to write her once a month while writing Elizabeth weekly.

Mama asks Elizabeth, "Do you want to start at the beginning and keep everything in chronological order, or do you want to pick birthday cards and Christmas cards first? And do you want to read your mother's letters at all, or do you want to leave them untouched?"

It seems silly to Elizabeth that she does not know the answer to those questions, but she doesn't. She doesn't know what she needs to know, much less what she wants to know. In the end, Elizabeth concludes that she probably needs to know it all. She has never liked leaving even one stone unturned. Perhaps, being thorough will bring closure to the years of bitterness, and healing to the scars left by so much confusion. Elizabeth is willing to apply every balm that the Lord gives her; which, in truth, is wrapped up in one thing, the faith to view it all in light of what the Lord has done for her.

They decide on chronological order, beginning with letters to a nine-year-old girl, which are sweet, and much the same, because Mama figured Elizabeth didn't read what was in the previous ones. They all include similar words of affirmation about how special she is and how much she is missed. The variable information often includes a story about their family, the church, a school friend or a town event. Sometimes there are pictures of the dog, the flowers or the house decorated for Christmas. In the cards, there is always money, a dollar bill in each while she is young and more as she reaches her teen years.

The information that she gathers from reading the letters is mostly about events that would not have interested her for long because she would have been too far removed in distance and time. But it provides her now with a great history of those ten years. The pictures bring a few tears to her eyes at what she has missed. On the other hand, encased in the letters is a comforting repetition. Week in and week out for ten long and unresponsive years, Mama never wavered in her devotion to Elizabeth and her desire that she stay on track with the Lord. Mama explains how she continued to find fresh ways to encourage.

"Why did you feel you needed fresh ways to encourage me since you knew I was not reading any of them?" Elizabeth asks.

Mama answers, "It was my way of keeping the love in me fresh, so that if I ever saw you again, I could express my love to you with the same fervency as I would if we had embraced every day of those ten years."

Through many cold wintry nights, Mama and Elizabeth keep up their pace. Eventually, Elizabeth opens the letters to her mother, also in the order they were sent, and finds them refreshingly loving from the beginning to the end. She is now unequivocally convinced that she has a durable heritage of abiding love.

Last year, she could not give her heart to anyone except her mother. She did not think she would ever be able to, but the letters are helping to dispel more areas of distrust. Mama's forthright personality and her impeccable timing on opening the box, in addition to her way of imparting acceptance, help Elizabeth to see that more seeds of trust are growing in her. But how long will that trust take to mature, and what route will it follow?

She decides to attend Moffat University in north Georgia, because its history of high academics coupled with student involvement make it seem like a place where Elizabeth would be comfortable. Its distance is such that she can come home occasionally, yet she will not be tempted to run to her new-found refuge on a whim.

"The Lord does not want me to forget," she reminds herself, "for even a nano second, that He is my real refuge."

Elizabeth will be leaving the first week of January, and she has shopping to do, friends to write, and houses to clean one more time before she goes.

Christmas passes in a calm and simple way that is soothing for Mama and Elizabeth. They need some quiet in their lives after the unleashed sentiment of the last six months. While working through so much, they have become best friends again, somewhat like they were when Elizabeth was young, except better, because now they are both women.

Before leaving for school, Elizabeth assesses her time since her mother's death. It began as an accumulation of baby steps, grew into regular steps and afforded occasional giant steps in learning more of walking well with the Savior. She appreciates the teachers and accountability partners, especially the Titus 2 women. They have fit the description of exhibiting holiness, not falsely accusing others, not becoming drunk with wine, and being teachers of good things. They have been diligent to train her in the ways of being sober, discreet, and chaste; and have taught her the ways of keeping a home, and of loving a husband and children, in the event that those become a part of her life. In wrapping up her self-assessment, she once more questions whether she is ready for another change.

# Chapter 9

Mama cries when Elizabeth leaves. Elizabeth cries, too. They know they are about to experience another ending. But, they also know they can much more easily handle an ending which promises another beginning. Mama writes more than once a week now, as she knows Elizabeth is getting her letters. She also knows the letters are encouraging Elizabeth, and that she will get a reply. Both guard this relationship that connects them beyond their ability to comprehend it.

Because she can, Elizabeth is taking a heavy course load. She loves to study. However, in order to catch up to her class, she must do two years in one, and she does not think that is necessary. She much prefers to have time to seek the Lord's face, through His word, on every issue of her life. There are men vying for her attention now, and she likes the excitement of it. She has waited a long time to be able to respond to those overtures, and believes she is at home enough in her soul to perhaps share a bit of a romantic relationship with someone else.

Mama loves it when Elizabeth visits alone, but she also delights in Elizabeth's friends, who come home with her. She enjoys the girls, but she especially likes watching Elizabeth's interaction with the guys. Mama is looking for signs that they know what they are doing, but also that Elizabeth knows what she is doing, and Mama is always pleased.

Elizabeth is sometimes home at the same time that Phillip is visiting Aunt Jan. They resume their friendship, having fun and meaningful times together. They promise to write, but somehow never get around to it, as they know they will eventually see each other again and catch up.

But, things will change now, as Phillip is finishing his final year at Emory and plans to spend the next year abroad working on an international degree. Elizabeth plans to stay at Moffat, methodically moving forward and remaining content. Will they write to each other now, or is their friendship one that can come and go at will?

Elizabeth's semester is ending, and she pronounces it good. She is on the Dean's List, making Mama proud, and she is certain that her parents would have been proud, also.

Elizabeth hasn't discussed her summer plans with Mama, though she knows there will not be a repeat of last year, because last summer was one of a kind. She does expect to hear that Mama will want her help again. So, when they speak on the phone next, she asks, "Mama, what do you have in mind for me this summer?"

The reply is too quick, "Whatever you have in mind for yourself."

Elizabeth wonders: Does she want me there or not? Is she afraid of hindering my growing up? Does she need her own space? I really thought we were past the caution and able to open up completely.

"Mama," she asks, "What do you have in mind?'

"Oh, Elizabeth, I want you to go forward and not feel like you need to be here as my little maid."

"Mama, what if I want to be your 'little maid,' for at least one more summer?"

Mama breathes an audible sigh and laughs. They are on for the summer.

Meanwhile, Elizabeth brings one last group home for a weekend, before beginning to study for exams. Mama knows most of them, but Suzette is new to her. She finds Suzette puzzling, which bothers Mama. She needs to have clear direction with people. After they all leave on Sunday, Mama realizes a piece of expensive costume jewelry is missing. Being someone who likes to think the best of people, and remembering a scene from Anne of Green Gables, in which Marilla accuses Anne of stealing her brooch and punishes her harshly, only to find it later, Mama decides not to mention the missing necklace.

The next week, at an end-of-the-year party on campus, Elizabeth notices and comments on a piece of Suzette's jewelry that looks exactly like one Mama has. Suzette seems mildly distracted, betraying the panic welling up inside her, and changes the subject, ending the conversation.

# Chapter 10

Sitting in the swing is how Elizabeth spends most of her first day at home. Summer, for her, is epitomized by feeling the breezes blow through the trees and across the porch, watching the hummingbirds, drinking lemonade, and enjoying the array of flowers in the yard. She is engulfed by comfort.

In the evening, while unpacking, Elizabeth finds Mama's necklace in her jewelry box. She knows that she did not put it there. She also knows it is the same one she had commented about to Suzette. Although she toys with the idea of slipping it back into Mama's room without saying anything, she thinks better of it, considering possible ramifications. If Mama has missed it already, it could lead her to think that Elizabeth had taken it. Honesty and integrity are not only about getting something back to its rightful owner, but also about being truly straightforward.

Elizabeth hands Mama the necklace, sharing the story, as she knows it. Elizabeth recognizes that she is blessed to have many mentors in Godly living, but what about Suzette? She asks Mama that question and Mama's reply is so typical of her. She simply states that she would like for Elizabeth to invite Suzette back next year, because she needs a second chance that may be life changing for her.

Mama explains, "It cannot hurt us if we temporarily or permanently, lose a piece or two of jewelry, but it can help Suzette if she sees the folly of her behavior and adopts a different way of life."

Mama teaches Elizabeth, in that instant, that they should take a chance on Suzette and on all the other Suzettes that will cross their paths.

Elizabeth agrees with Mama, then thinks aloud as she makes her way down the hallway to her room, "The safety of home is such a warm blanket on a cold night, such a cool breeze on a hot day, such a positive triumph over a negative possibility. Oh, why do I try to be poetic? The safety of home is the safety of home. It is plain and simple. And I don't know anyone who enjoys the safety of home more than I do. I am so blessed."

The summer passes quickly with the jam making, canning and freezing, in addition to Elizabeth's classes in the art of life while doing her volunteer cleaning.

Before leaving for England, Phillip comes for one last visit. They enjoy their usual casual time together, though this time he seems to have something on his mind that he never quite articulates. He seems unsettled somehow. She attributes it to his being a little nervous about the coming year and all the new adventures, but wonders if it could be something more?

# Chapter 11

There is a nip in the air on the day Elizabeth moves back into the dorm for the fall semester at Moffat, a place where the leaves seem to outdo themselves every year. She is immediately struck by the void left in the absence of her friends who have graduated, and the ones who chose, for whatever reason, not to return. But she enjoys meeting the new crop of freshmen and transfers, and looks for a few who seem lost and in need of a friend. She looks for Suzette, since she is to be Mama's special friend in the coming year. Elizabeth does not find her the first day and her heart sinks. It seems to Elizabeth that Suzette needs her Mama. It turns out that Suzette did not come back, so Elizabeth and Mama keep her in their prayers, not knowing all her needs, but believing that the Holy Spirit can and will interpret those prayers to their proper needs.

On the first day of orientation, Elizabeth is called into the office, and to her surprise, finds a beautiful and charismatic young lady flashing sparkling eyes and a ready smile in her direction. She is especially engaging, so engaging that the wheelchair, which carries her from place to place, is hardly noticeable. She lost her leg, just above the knee, from a boating accident last year near her home in south Florida. Her very life was hanging in the balance for weeks. Next came the surgeries to repair what they could. The physical healing time was coupled with the emotional pain of losing a leg and the rejection of losing a boyfriend.

Young people tend to think their first high school love will be the love of their life; but though that does occasionally happen, it is rarely the case. When hard times come at such a young age, people tend to deal with them only if they are forced to, not because they choose to. Sometimes, even when forced, they don't rise well to the occasion. But that is not true of Jeannie.

She is driven in positive ways. She needs help, though, maneuvering around this lovely campus of rolling hills. Why had she chosen it, as opposed to one in a big city with easier accessibility for her wheelchair? Well, they will find that out when and if she decides to tell them. For now, Elizabeth is standing before Jeannie because she has been chosen to acclimate her to campus life by carrying her books, helping her on elevators, and generally seeing that life works well for her. Elizabeth expects the campus administration did not ask her in private, because they knew she could not resist Jeannie's charisma once she saw her. The truth is that if they had not asked her, she would have volunteered.

As time passes, Elizabeth delight's in their growing friendship. Elizabeth defines Jeannie as having "a spunk that was never mine," as she laughs at the vicarious experiences she lives out through Jeannie's detailed and enthralling descriptions.

Jeannie is here for only one semester while her leg heals, and she capitalizes on her new environment that provides more fodder for her continually waiting audience. Next semester, she will be fitted for a walking prosthesis and will need to be near her doctor back home for the constant fine-tuning and the physical therapy required for her to learn how to walk properly again.

Elizabeth's mind drifts to the possibilities, and she thinks to herself: My guess is that by the time she graduates, she will walk across the stage without anyone ever detecting her handicap. Already, she reminds me of a racehorse spared from the glue factory by some benevolent owner who would nurse him back to health and train him for the fun of it, only to find he has a horse with a winner's heart and much to other people's surprise, a winner's legs. We have all heard the stories of those who excel out of hardship. In fact, much human excellence seems to be born out of hardship. So, we should not be surprised when it happens before our very eyes to this determined young woman.

Jeannie is undaunted; nothing seems too large a task for her. So when Elizabeth asks if she wants to come to Mama's for a weekend, Jeannie jumps at the chance. While there, she meets Aunt Jan who shows her pictures of Phillip and tells her all about his continental schooling. Through that brief bit of information, Jeannie decides that he is the man for Elizabeth, who laughs and explains that they are soul mates on a friendship level.

Mama falls in love with Jeannie, and begs her to come back before the semester ends. Elizabeth can understand that Mama is drawn to Jeannie's bubbling personality, but there is also a camaraderie that Elizabeth cannot explain. This she knows, though, that Mama will explain it to her in due time. Living with Mama is a little microcosm of what it is like walking with God. You must trust and wait.

Elizabeth hears often from Phillip and thinks he is quite homesick in the mother country. All of his letters are considered, by Jeannie, to be a signs of Phillip's undying affection for Elizabeth. But when Elizabeth lets Jeannie read them and asks her to point to something in them that leads her to that conclusion, Jeannie cannot.

Elizabeth thinks: Jeannie is a hopeless romantic. Perhaps, I should fix the two of them up as soon as they are in Erwin at the same time.

# Chapter 12

At Thanksgiving, Mama insists on inviting Jeannie's family up to spend the holiday with them, rather than having her fly home. Since Jeannie has two siblings who are much younger, it is an easy trip to arrange. Her family arrives at the Nashville airport about the time Elizabeth and Jeannie arrive at Mama's, so they have a couple of hours to settle in and get ready for the Greenes' arrival.

Jeannie and Elizabeth pick whatever is growing in the yard and make fall decorations for the table. Jeannie is impressed at Elizabeth's creativity, and Elizabeth knows, at that moment, that Jeannie must meet her older and wiser friends on this trip.

Elizabeth also thinks it might be a good time to get out the letters that her father had received just before his death. The memory of them has recently surfaced for some unknown reason. Will she even be able to find them? Everything from that time was either thrown away or stored at Mama's. Surely, they are stored at Mama's. After all, they would mean as much to her as they would to Elizabeth.

Jeannie, Mama, and Elizabeth all rush to the door when they hear a car drive up. Jeannie's parents hug their daughter, then Mama and Elizabeth as if they are family, too. Mama likes that, because everyone is family to her. The children had noticed from the road as they approached the house that even though the front porch has a railing around it, the back one does not. They can't wait to jump off the side of it, the way Elizabeth had done as a little girl, but has not done since her return. Watching them, Elizabeth cannot resist.

"Ouch!" she shouts, "I twisted my ankle."

Mama is worried, but Elizabeth is confident it is only a sprain. Mr. Greene scoops her up and carries her inside. After settling her on the couch in the den and elevating her leg with a pillow, he begins to examine the foot and ankle.

Jeannie laughs at the puzzled expressions, and says, "Just being the CEO at a teaching hospital does not make someone a doctor. But in this case, the CEO is not only a doctor, he is also an orthopedic doctor."

Immediately Dr. Greene pronounces Elizabeth's amateur diagnosis as correct. It is indeed a sprain, and must be elevated and an ice pack placed on it for the next couple of hours. That means Elizabeth will not be going to the attic for her father's letters on this trip. Suddenly, she realizes it was wrong timing anyway to get them out with company around, since they were meant to be private.

Jeannie, the kids, and Elizabeth settle in for a long game of Monopoly. The game gets loud and the happy sounds bring Aunt Jan over to join the fun. She brings pictures of Phillip at all of England's major historical places. Elizabeth especially likes the one of him standing in front of the palace, wearing an exaggerated tourist outfit and holding a sign that says, "My Vacation Home." Phillip has always been thoughtful and sensitive, but she had thought his sense of humor needed tweaking. Perhaps she was wrong.

Elizabeth simultaneously realizes two things: That he hasn't written to her for a while and that she is viewing a picture of Phillip holding hands with a lovely British girl.

Why, she wonders, does her heart feel as though it is sinking, when she should only be thrilled?

Jeannie is obviously not thrilled, but is discreet in her comments.

Soon, their chili and grilled cheese sandwich supper is ready, and Elizabeth joins the others at the dining table where she props her foot up and enjoys the family gathering. They talk like there is no tomorrow, sharing family stories.

Jeannie tells them that she was adopted when she was four. She has slight memories of her birth parents. She mostly remembers that her mother was truly a beauty queen. Wait! She admits that maybe she remembers the beauty part from the one picture her family has. Jeannie tries to tell the story, but begins to choke up. Her parents say that is a story for another time, because tonight is not for crying. Now, Elizabeth is curious, but she also understands and respects their privacy.

The smells of apple and pecan pies waft into the bedroom as the sun streams in through the skylight overhead. What a wonderful way to wake up. Elizabeth thinks as she dresses and then hobbles down the hall to see who else is already up. She is surprised to see that they all are. She stretches and relaxes again as she sees that Mrs. Greene has usurped her position in the kitchen, beside Mama. Elizabeth reminisces about her mother and Mama working in the kitchen together on those holidays gone by.

Holidays are bittersweet, she privately surmises. They are filled with fun and hope intermingled with memories, both good and bad. I praise the Lord that He is able to take the bad and put it into His eternal perspective for those who know Him. I long to know my parents and be with them like Jeannie is with hers. But wait, she only knows those who are her parents now. She doesn't have even the memories that I have. As I think back through the years, Daddy fills my mind with joy, and Mommy fills my mind with a clouded kind of love. I see that she was plagued with the demons and unrest of not being saved. They drove her to such desperation. Yet, in her desperation, she found the Lord in the nick of time. Yes, the holidays remind me that this world is not all there is. They remind me that my mother is on an eternal holiday with the Lord. I feel the joy, and, yes, the joy has far exceeded the pain.

Dr. Greene asks the young people if they want to go for a ride. The kids decline, opting to stay home and jump off the porch. It is a game to them to see who can jump the farthest, and the good thing is that there is a doctor in the house.

Jeannie and Elizabeth make their way to the family's wheelchair-equipped van and settle in. Dr. Greene begins to drive as if he knows where he is going. Elizabeth asks if he has ever been to Erwin before, or if he just has a keen sense of direction. He replies that he has actually been here before, concerning one of his cases many years ago. He knows where the hospital is. As they drive through the countryside, Elizabeth and Jeannie spot more fall foliage, some of which they insist on gathering. Rather, they insist on having Dr. Greene gather it for them, and he accommodates.

Upon returning, the girls make more fall floral decorations. And, since it is still several hours until dinnertime, they persuade Dr. Greene to be their delivery driver, taking the arrangements to Mrs. Bach, Mrs. Carter, and Mrs. Sims. They only stay a short time at each place, but it is enough for Jeannie to know that she wants more, and they promise to come back later during the weekend.

Dinner is the best ever, but Elizabeth thinks that after most every meal Mama fixes. Mrs. Greene writes down some of Mama's recipes while the young people continue an extended game of Monopoly. Elizabeth sighs in the extreme comfort of this day.

Since her sprain is only slight, she finds that keeping her ankle elevated, all the time that she is not hobbling somewhere, has kept the swelling and pain at bay. Dr. Greene says she must still favor it for a while when she goes back to the hills of north Georgia, and she commits to follow the doctor's orders. That commitment will be easier to keep, she thinks, since Jeannie has learned to get around so well there without much help. Actually, Jeannie is so well liked that, if she needs help, students are practically fighting to assist her. With those instructions out of the way, they return to the freedom of being on break. Mama puts on coffee and music, finishing the picture of a happy house filled with happy people. It is truly Thanksgiving.

One thing that Mama consistently has done since Elizabeth was a little girl is to put up Christmas decorations the day after Thanksgiving. Because she wants the season's decor to last long, she uses an artificial tree. But this year, the young people beg for a real one, too, even if it loses all its needles by the middle of December.

"Two trees?" Mama asks.

"Yes!" They shout in unison.

Dr. Greene knows his job assignment and is already out in the shed looking for an axe and the other equipment he will need. Mama is calling her brother who lives on a farm, about twelve miles from town, to ask if he has seen any suitable trees this year and if she can send a crew out to get one.

She receives a "yes" answer to both questions.

This time, the adventure sounds much more exciting to the kids than jumping off the porch. So they are off, singing Christmas carols as they go into the day, which is cold enough to get everyone in the mood, but not so piercing as to take the fun away.

Uncle Jimmy, having learned from Mama of Jeannie's mobility situation, as well as Elizabeth's, knows just where to direct them within fifty feet of that perfect tree. Jeannie will hear of nothing less than that her father wheel her to the spot before he begins cutting. This perfect tree is at least six feet tall and ideally rounded, except for one gaping hole.

"Toward the wall," they say in unison, and Dr. Greene begins to saw. The kids take turns sawing and find it more difficult than fun. Laughter erupts over this new experience for them all. They forgot the camera, but it is a scene that not any of them will soon forget. And with Jeannie's story-telling skills, all who hear will have a vivid mind picture.

After caring for two semi-invalids in the woods, then cutting and dragging a huge cedar tree and securing it to the top of the van with Uncle Jimmy's help, Dr. Greene longs for a nap. But, everyone knows that a fresh-cut tree takes much more set up time and energy than an artificial one. So his job is not nearly finished.

He trims the sappy branches as their sharp needles prick and pierce him. He takes the challenge to make it stand straight in the mostly worn-out stand from the garage, while laughing, and admitting to all that making these memories far exceeds the fleeting pleasure of dozing by the flickering fire. Besides, he knows that there is a long night's sleep on the horizon to prepare him for tomorrow's events.

# Chapter 13

Saturday brings a heavy frost resembling a light snow. The Florida kids are thrilled as they rush out to take pictures and try to gather enough frost to make a frost ball.

In the afternoon, the plan is to visit the older ladies again. Jeannie and Elizabeth thought they would go alone, but for some reason, Dr. Greene expresses a serious interest in going along, especially to Mrs. Carter's.

They make their rounds and have leftover Thanksgiving dessert at each place. Arriving at Mrs. Carter's last, and being quite stuffed, they feel duty-bound to eat her mincemeat pie. They do, however, get to wash it down with her famous boiled custard, Elizabeth's favorite dessert treat of the entire holiday season. The girls load the dirty dishes on a tray, and Jeannie carries it to the kitchen on her lap, with Elizabeth pushing the wheelchair while hobbling along. There, they are captivated by Mrs. Carter's aquarium of tropical fish, and they lose track of time.

Meanwhile, Dr. Greene asks Mrs. Carter about a small, framed photo on her piano.

She explains, "This is our only child, our lovely daughter,

who died following a car accident in south Florida where she lived with her husband, a medical equipment salesman, and their young daughter. She had survived for weeks after the accident, her broken bones were beginning to heal and her pain was growing less, when, without warning, a blood clot broke loose and went to her heart. Within minutes, she was dead.

"Her husband was distraught, but tried to keep home and hearth together. However, having a traveling job, he soon realized that he could not care for a little one. I had stayed all of the time during Susie's hospitalization. After the funeral, I traveled back and forth for three months, helping with the care of my precious grandchild. I pleaded with Jim to let us bring her here for a while.

"Instead, he decided to turn her over to the attending physician on Susie's case, who had no children and was looking to adopt. Jim loved the way the physician and his daughter interacted. He knew that she would live a privileged life in a wonderful Christian home."

With measured speech, she continues, "We asked for visitation, but Jim said that he wanted her to experience a complete integration into her new family, and not to be torn and shuffled around. Back then, grandparents had no recourse. He, being the father, had all the rights to give her up with no input from us."

"We lost our daughter to tragedy and we lost our granddaughter to wrong thinking. But, I have photos and memories. You have been looking at my favorite photo of Susie on the piano."

She pauses, "For some reason, I have a feeling that you recognize her, and it is not by coincidence that you are in my house at this very moment. Dr. Greene, this story is intimately familiar to you, isn't it?"

He slowly answers, "Yes," and hangs his head in silence.

Mrs. Carter speaks softly, "This could be an awkward moment for both of us, but I want to dispel that as quickly as I can."

She calmly continues, "I had long ago given up hope of ever knowing my grandchild, yet, when I met her a few days ago, I knew her! The physical features and the mannerism are succinct, and the time frame fits. I have had long enough to sort through the facts, as I know them. I observed, almost instantly, the joy on Jeannie's face, the excitement in her personality, the care with which she is handled, and the hope in her heart. Her life has been abundantly blessed through the years. Mine has been blessed at seeing her again. I carry no grudge over losing her. I know how to forgive. I am continually learning from the One who has forgiven me all."

Dr. Greene cannot speak for the uncontrollable sobs that catch in his throat and shake his body. He has loved the Lord and walked well with him for his entire adult life, yet never has he known anyone other than the LORD Himself with such complete forgiveness. And she is the grandmother of his child. He composes himself, softly walks to her chair, and stoops to one knee before her, where he takes her hands in his and thanks her with all the gratitude he knows how to express.

She pats his shoulder and they know they are inextricably bonded for life, in an instant that they will never be able to explain. It is theirs and theirs alone, yet the outflow of it will change the future of every family member.

Dr. Greene has figured out that company is always welcome at Mama's, so he invites "Grandma" Carter to go back with them to share the astounding news. While he goes to the bathroom to wash his face, she gathers pictures from her keepsake box, and the girls return from the kitchen with crosstitch towels, announcing that they want to learn to make them.

Upon their arrival, Mama is surprised and pleased to see her good friend coming to be part of their evening. She quickly runs to the kitchen, puts on a pot of coffee, and returns to find everyone seated around the dining table. Mrs. Carter and Dr. Greene are the only ones not wearing puzzled expressions.

The two of them look at each other and say simultaneously, "Who wants to begin?"

Then each replies, "I do."

Everyone laughs and begs for someone to begin.

Mrs. Carter decides to lay all her pictures on the table, pictures that include Susie at every stage of her life, until her death at age twenty-seven. Also in the growing tabletop collage are pictures of Jeannie from babyhood to age four.

Each one at the table sees different pictures first, and each registers different reactions. All in the Greene family recognize the pictures of Jeannie as similar to ones that her father had given them. Mrs. Greene sees immediately that Jeannie looks strikingly like the beautiful daughter of Mrs. Carter. Mama had recognized the resemblance the first time she saw Jeannie, which is what spurred her invitation for Thanksgiving in the first place. Mama's theory is that you don't know if you don't ask, which was her eventual plan if all else failed. Since Dr. Greene had remembered the trip to Erwin for records all those years ago, he viewed the invitation as providential.

After laughs and hugs and tears and establishing that Mrs. Carter would from this day forward be called "Grandma," the family settles down to put together each minute detail of the past. Their future begins now, and will establish itself well when Grandma flies with Jeannie to Florida for Christmas.

# Chapter 14

Back at school, John, who has had his eye on Elizabeth all semester, musters up his courage and asks her to the school Christmas banquet. She excitedly accepts, but Jeannie is not happy, as she is holding out to see Phillip and Elizabeth as a couple.

"Well, Phillip is in England, so he surely can't escort me to this party," Elizabeth says, trying to sort things out in her own mind. "Besides, the last I know of him is that he is tenderly holding another girl's hand. In addition, haven't we been established as only great friends? Is Jeannie never going to let me enjoy a date? Will she at least help me pick out an exquisite dress?"

Later, and under duress, Jeannie helps Elizabeth get ready for the banquet.

Elizabeth stands before the full-length mirror and gives herself permission to say, "I look lovely."

Her date finds her a breathtaking sight in the perfectly styled gold brocade dress with a fitted bodice and slightly full skirt. The black velvet wrap and the red rosebud corsage are the finishing touches.

Though her ankle seems healed, she is walking a little

wobbly in high-heeled shoes, inspiring John to steady her with the ideal amount of attentiveness. The food is not the usual Hamilton cafeteria fare, and being entertained by the faculty band and comedy team helps the students to see their instructors as ordinary people.

"Thank you, John, for a delightful evening," Elizabeth says as they arrive at the dorm steps.

"You are welcome," he responds with no hint of waiting for a goodnight kiss. And, though she has had a wonderful time, she is relieved that there is no expectation on his part.

Later, Jeannie says, "Elizabeth, you did not want him to kiss you because you have your heart set on Phillip."

Elizabeth rolls her eyes as she asks, " Will you ever give up?"

Elizabeth knows she will miss Jeannie terribly when her friend is in Florida being fitted for and learning to use her prosthesis during the next semester. Elizabeth wishes she could be there, observing her progress. She is sure Jeannie will turn the rehab center upside down with her antics, and they will love her, as everyone does.

Grandma will be there, taking pictures and keeping a diary to share. She has blossomed with having her granddaughter as her dear friend, so much like Mama and Elizabeth. Mrs. Greene, whose mother went to be with the Lord when Jeannie was only seven, has also taken Grandma as her own. The happiness that radiates between two states is contagious, with more to come.

# Chapter 15

Christmas break is definitely welcomed by Elizabeth. Even though she enjoyed her heavy load, she is exhausted and has been plagued with a slight sore throat since returning to school after Thanksgiving. Elizabeth thinks some rest will alleviate that generally rundown feeling, but Mama sends her straight to the doctor, ignoring Elizabeth's protests.

Her doctor's visit reveals mononucleosis, and the treatment will keep her in bed during Christmas break, staying warm and drinking lots of fluids. Well, Elizabeth thinks, isn't staying in bed what she had already planned to do? Yes, but she wanted it to be her choice! Mama is sad that Elizabeth is ill, but she loves waiting on her, and Elizabeth loves being waited on by Mama, a luxury not afforded her through their years of separation.

Fortunately, they diagnosed her illness in its early stages, and the doctor thinks that if Elizabeth is a good patient and follows his instructions to rest, that she can go back to school in January. She is glad, since she does not want to interrupt her schooling again.

Spending much of her time on the couch in the den, she is mesmerized by the sparkling Christmas lights and comforted by the treasured family ornaments decorating the real tree. Mama kept it watered and did not turn its lights on it until Elizabeth came home, in hopes of saving its freshness for her to enjoy. Though she is confined to the bed and couch, she is enjoying the books Mama brings her from the library, as well as the continual replaying of the Thanksgiving events in her head. The replays help her to solidify good and happy memories in her own life.

It reminds her of Philippians 4:8 in the Scriptures, "Finally brethren, whatsoever things are true, whatsoever things are honest, whatsoever things are just, whatsoever things are pure, whatsoever things are lovely, whatsoever things are of good report; if there be any virtue, and if there be any praise, think on these things." She wishes she would not ever again get caught in the trap of thinking on things that don't edify, for things that don't edify seem to distort the truth and drag a person down. Minds become fixated, and it is hard to see past the fixation. She sees it in Jen at school. Jen loves the Lord, but her mind seems distracted and her countenance whispers uncertainty.

"Lord, do you want to use me to encourage her in the purity of your freedom?" Elizabeth asks. "If so, please prepare me during this time of rest."

The tree lights have been turned off when Elizabeth awakens, wondering how long she has been asleep on the couch. As she squints to see her watch, she notices a little daylight peeking through the edge of the blinds. It is morning. She has slept since supper. If she does this often enough, surely her body will heal quickly and be strong.

As she picks up her Bible and looks for scriptures that show who we are and what we have in Christ, she asks herself: Is that where I need to begin with Jen?

"Oh, Lord, thank you that even if you do not use me in Jen's life, you are preparing my very own heart to stand firm in the midst of wrong thinking." Elizabeth speaks softly.

# Chapter 16

Elizabeth feels refreshed and ready to tackle a new term. However, the doctor has asked her to drop two classes and to rest throughout the day as well as in the evenings. She agrees, thinking it should be easier to follow his directions, since she does not have her friend, Jeannie, the social butterfly, to keep her on the run this semester.

There seem to have been many transfers, resulting in an absence of familiar faces. Elizabeth does not see John. When she asks about him, she finds that he is again dating his former girlfriend of many years and they decided to attend their local state school together.

Elizabeth looks for Jen and finds her sitting alone under a tree, crying. Gently putting her arm around Jen's shoulder, she waits. Jen finally looks at her and musters a faint smile. Elizabeth asks if she can be a listening ear, and Jen opens up with a deluge. The words come so fast and the thoughts are so scattered that Elizabeth is having a hard time picking out any one of the many intertwined stories. She slides around to face Jen and holds her hand as she listens and listens. Elizabeth suspects that Jen will perhaps not hear her in the midst of this much emotion, so she does not speak. She allows Jen to spend her emotions until she is weak and limp and gasping for breath.

They look straight at each other and Jen asks, "Can you help me?"

Elizabeth answers, "I know the One who can."

Jen looks scared as she tells Elizabeth that she also knows the One who can, but it doesn't seem like He wants to help her, concerning all the things she just shared.

Elizabeth asks her to read the scripture that personally comforted her immensely over the break, Philippians 4:8, knowing well that sometimes when a person is inundated with wrong thoughts, such an answer could seem abrasive, as though spoken by someone who does not understand the depths of agony. Yet, she knows that scripture holds the answers. She then asks Jen to meet her the next day for lunch and a drive, a plan which gives time for Jen's emotions to settle, and time for Elizabeth to search those scriptures, and implore the Lord to show her the specific wisdom from them that will speak to Jen and her situation.

Having three more days before classes begin and doing no extra-curricular activities this semester gives Elizabeth ample time to focus on Jen. She is rested and ready when they meet. After eating in the cafeteria, they head for Elizabeth's sun-drenched car. It feels good to have the rays streaming through the windows, comfortably warming them on this nippy fall day.

Elizabeth says, "This reminds me of how the Son of God can warm and brighten our hearts in a similar way."

She waits until she sees Jen's attention focused on her, and then explains, "The car did nothing to soak up the sun's warmth and pass it on to others except to be in the sun's presence. It can happen to our hearts and minds in the same way. We simply put ourselves in the Lord's presence, through His word, and wait. Sometimes we want to sort out all that is happening to us in ways that we plan. Only when our plan is in tune with His Biblical plan can we be sure that our plan is right. Therefore, if only His plan is right and we want to be right, we must use His plan, part of which is that we do not get stuck in extrapolating small bits and pieces of scripture and applying them like bandages. He wants us to know Him! He wants us to walk with Him, to trust Him, and to depend on Him. He wants to be our all. When He is our all, it changes our vision and we can see our situation through His perfection, forgiveness, and love.

"Conversely, when we look through our little pinhole of personal hurt, we see only that hurt and we see it magnified and distorted. The answer is not to keep focusing on those problems and trying to fix them, so we can feel better. The answer lies in solidifying the truth of who we are in Christ, and filtering all of life's experiences through that love relationship of being fully accepted and complete in Him.

"I can never keep up with the things I want to fix in someone else concerning their wrongs to me. By the same token," Elizabeth adds with a smile and a wink, "as nice as I think I am, others cannot keep up with all they want to fix about me, concerning them. That is because we are not the fixers. In this life, it is Christ Jesus who takes us as we are, and fixes our character through our grateful obedience to Him. It is part of our Christian walk with the Lord, really the essence of our walk with Him, that we are growing in the grace that is ours."

Following a short silence, Elizabeth asks, " Jen, will you do a project with me?

"Yes," she replies, a bit unsure.

"I want us to read through Paul's epistles, one chapter a day, and make note cards of entire verses that show us how important we are to the Lord. Every day, we will share those verses with each other. Perhaps we will memorize them. Finally, we will put each one in a strategic place, where it will be seen often by us. This is designed to change our thought patterns to be in tune with the Lord of Lords. Don't ask me to help you with any of the problems that poured out of your emotions yesterday, until we have done this project consistently through the end of spring break, almost three months from now.

Do we have a deal?"

"Yes," Jen answers, this time with a hint of confidence.

Elizabeth sees this project as one way the Lord is using to focus her own life more diligently on Him, especially once her classes begin.

Art appreciation is Elizabeth's favorite class, mainly because her professor is not only artsy, which she enjoys, but he also has a dry sense of humor. She finds herself chuckling over his subtle comments after everyone else is back to the lesson.

"Perhaps," she thinks, "I am really British and don't know it." Thinking of the British reminds her of Phillip and how very long it has been since she has heard from him. She will get another letter out to him this afternoon.

As she drops her letter off, she finds a note in her mailbox to pick up a package at the main window, and licks her lips in anticipation of homemade cookies.

At the window, she meets a transfer student from Australia, who has the most authentic Australian accent she has ever heard; actually, the only one she has ever heard in person. As he gives her the package, she continues to engage him in conversation, just to hear his voice, eventually asking him if he can teach her to sound like an Aussie.

"Do you want to begin tonight?" he questions.

"Of course," she answers, and they arrange to meet for dinner in the cafeteria at 5:30.

Elizabeth notices her package is from Jeannie and rips it open. She finds a keychain with a miniature prosthesis that has working parts, like hers.

"What a conversation piece," she says to herself.

"What a conversation piece," her new Aussie friend says.

Suddenly, two things occur to her. The first is that the two of them must think alike, and the second is that she does not know his name.

As she turns to leave, she says, "When you get to the cafeteria tonight, you will be looking for a girl named Elizabeth."

"Yes," he replies, "I know your name from the package."

There is a prolonged silence, and Elizabeth realizes that he is not going to share his name. She smiles because she likes his little game.

Her first lesson in Aussie is funnier than it is productive, but isn't that the real purpose anyway? She had wondered who would make her laugh this term, since Jeannie is gone. And, she has her answer. At the end of their meeting, they make arrangements for another lesson, same time and same place tomorrow night.

Just for fun, Elizabeth says, "When you get to the cafeteria, you will be looking for a girl named Elizabeth, carrying a working prosthesis key chain."

Again there is silence. Again she smiles as they leave in separate directions.

Before bedtime that evening, she calls Jeannie and finds that she has been fitted with her prosthesis. It is a bit heavier than she had expected, but Jeannie is optimistic, especially since her therapists are the masters at encouragement. In addition, Jeannie shares that the family plans to accompany Grandma home for Easter, so the girls will see each other then.

"Perhaps we will take a walk together," Jeannie gushes.

Elizabeth laughs and says, "Perhaps we will run a race."

Meeting Jen for lunch and her Aussie friend for dinner on a daily basis keeps Elizabeth on her toes spiritually and comically, and she is enjoying both.

Jen is a fanatic about doing the homework Elizabeth assigned her, which prompts Elizabeth to say to her, "Lighten up and enjoy the Lord."

They have both memorized two new verses this week, and have many taped in interesting places. Jen has one on her bathroom mirror, of course. Some are marking the upcoming lesson of each textbook. The best is that she puts the one she thinks she needs the most on her stash of chocolate. Elizabeth knows that for Jen to hide God's word in her heart cannot fail, and that thinking on things that are good, pure, true, and kind is a consistently comforting way to live.

    For now, this project seems to be more work than pleasure for Jen. Soon, Elizabeth expects to see more peace on her face. She is looking for a vibrant personality to come out of hiding. Elizabeth sometimes wishes she could speed the process for Jen, but she understands that the progress and the timetable are not hers.

    After one month of faithfully keeping her lunch and dinner dates, Elizabeth notices that Jen's demeanor is much calmer and her voice quality no longer sounds strained. Elizabeth is pleased to see evidence of the Lord working in her friend, but their plan is still to not discuss the particulars with each other until after spring break.

    The Aussie is really named Morgan Price, which Elizabeth found out from a friend who works in the admissions office. But Morgan has never told her, so they are still playing their game. Her Aussie accent and vocabulary are improving. Still, these encounters are mostly about laughing. The flip side is that she is teaching him how to speak a little bit of "rural South" which, in Elizabeth's case, is lacking in purity, being amusingly combined with the residual of her New York accent.

    Since it is Valentine's Day, Elizabeth fully expects a package from Mama. At the post office, "No Name" gives her not one, but two packages. One is, as she expected, a box of homemade cookies, which is shared with everyone in the vicinity. The other has no return address, but inside is a lovely heart shaped flower vase and a card signed, Morgan.

    Elizabeth shows it to "No Name," and exclaims, "Look, it is from my boyfriend back home." They have their best laugh ever. It is the perfect ending to their many weeks of joking about his name. She can now call him Morgan, and she likes that as much as she liked the joke.

Time passes quickly and spring break is just around the corner. Morgan is going to travel to New York City to see some of America's history. He is a maverick and has no problem striking out on his own. After all, he came to college in America, knowing no one.

Elizabeth is longing to see Jeannie. They email often, but Jeannie keeps her progress with the prosthesis a secret. Elizabeth does not dare to pressure for more information, because she wants to be surprised at how far Jeannie has come. Elizabeth's mind drifts to Mama's insight concerning Jeannie. It still amazes her how Mama suspected who Jeannie was from the first time they met.

Elizabeth wonders aloud, "Will I ever have the insight that Mama has or is she a phenomenon?" Even as Elizabeth asks herself that question, she has no idea how much insight Mama truly possesses.

## Chapter 17

The drive home is breathtaking, with newly planted spring annuals dotting lawns, azaleas blooming profusely, and dogwoods being the showstopper. Elizabeth pulls to the curb and asks a passerby to take her picture in front of a pink dogwood, in hopes it will be suitable to frame and give to Mama for Mother's Day. As she returns to her car and continues her ride through town, it occurs to her that every house she passes has a family unique unto itself, while also experiencing the ordinary ups and downs of life. And, it reminds her of the few of her father's letters that she read before he died. She wonders if someone else took over his anonymous benevolence in Erwin, and if there is such a person in this town and the next town and the next town.

The reunion at Grandma's house is as much of a renewal for Grandma as it is for Jeannie. Mama says that Grandma's house once was the place for parties. She was a grand hostess and her husband, Grey, was a grand host. But, when Susie and Jeannie were gone from their lives, the sparkle drained from their eyes. Though Grandma never lost her zeal for walking well with the Lord, there was an emptiness concerning family that now is being filled again. Of course, they miss Grey, but a revival of parties has begun and promises to be glorious. Tonight is the walk that they have all been waiting for.

Mama and Elizabeth arrive early so Mama can help in the kitchen and Elizabeth can put the finishing touches on the table arrangement, which she made earlier from fresh flowers out of Mama's yard. Jeannie is in her bedroom waiting for the clock to strike 7:00. No one gets a glimpse of the honored guest until then, when she will make her grand entrance, like Cinderella at the ball. She will be the princess.

Much to everyone's surprise, when Elizabeth knocks on Jeannie's door at five minutes until 7:00, there is no answer. After several knocks and still no answer, Mrs. Greene tries the door and finds it locked. She panics while Grandma grins, sheepishly. At that moment, they hear an unrelenting car horn in front of the house.

Everyone runs to the windows and then out onto the wraparound porch to see a white limousine pulling up. Dr. Greene steps out and, with exaggerated flair, opens the back door to allow Jeannie's siblings, Judith and Jake, to exit and run up the sidewalk announcing excitedly, "The princess is here! The princess is here!"

Meanwhile, Dr. Greene extends his hand as Jeannie gracefully slides her leg out of the car, and then gently lifts her prosthesis into position. Beaming as she takes her father's steadying hand, she begins her walk of fame, past the waiting crowd, which by now is lining the sidewalk and cheering wildly.

Throughout the evening, Jeannie shares stories of her rehab successes and setbacks. She notes that it often seemed like three steps forward and two steps back, but isn't that the way much of life is? The point is that the move was clearly forward and the outcome is unquestionable increments of success.

At the end of the evening, Jeannie pays a tribute to all who have sacrificed to make her road so much easier to travel. Her highest praises go to her family and closest friends, because they lifted not only her body, but also her spirit. Next, she reveals her plan to step aside as the girl with immediate needs, the high-maintenance one, and defer to Judith and Jake, the patient ones.

With so much behind them, Dr. and Mrs. Greene begin to reflect on the turn of events that brought them to Grandma and the ways in which their lives have changed for the better. They wonder if the same things could happen if they found Judith's and Jake's birth parents or whether, as they have been warned so many times, pursuing it could likely open a can of worms. For now, that is a question for another day.

# Chapter 18

Approaching campus, the first person Elizabeth sees is Jen sitting under the same tree where they initially became friends. Although she cannot see Jen's face, her body appears slumped. Elizabeth parks and rushes over to hug her, hoping that she has read the body language incorrectly. So, what a relief it is when she approaches and notices that Jen is hunched over her journal, writing. They exchange warm smiles, and Jen cannot wait any longer to catch Elizabeth up with what is going on in her life. She spills out words one over the other, much like the first time they met; but this time, her face is not strained and her voice does not crack. Again, Elizabeth listens and listens.

Jen tells Elizabeth that while she was home, she faced a young man who had lied about her morally and spread vicious gossip around her small town. Her reputation was smeared. Her parents did not want to believe the lies, but eventually they lost trust in her, also. She stops the story to thank Elizabeth for showing her where a girl goes when she cannot even go to her parents. She has spent her time this semester with the One who knows the whole truth, and she has found Him faithful.

The young man admitted to her that it was all part of a plan by several of his friends to ruin the reputations of innocent girls. She was their first victim. Seeing what it did to her, they have since disbanded their club, but they did not know how to rectify the damage done to her without getting themselves into serious trouble.

Oh, how Jen wants her good and hard-earned reputation back, but only God can do that. Through her study, she has come to see that God can and will restore anything He needs to be restored in order to use her the way He wants to use her. Does all of life now become easy? It does not, but it becomes more exciting and more clear.

Jen and Elizabeth both know that they must keep their study going. Getting over a huge hump, or walking through a long, dry spell, and coming out victorious does not mean that a person has arrived forever. It means that new challenges to walking well are on the horizon.

Elizabeth shares with Jen a conversation that she and Mama have occasionally, during which Mama says, "If I live to be 90, the good Lord will still be teaching me more things and walking me through suffering in His sufficiency."

Elizabeth explains that she always laughs and asks, "What happens, Mama, if you live to be 100?"

And Mama replies, "Same."

After unpacking, Elizabeth runs by the post office to see if there is any mail from the administration about her summer project, and there is. The project has been put on hold for undisclosed reasons. She considers that her opportunity to spend another summer with Mama. With next year being her senior year, tl could very well be her last summer at home.

    Things are status quo with Morgan. They see each other a dinner and campus activities and they laugh incessantly, but they make no plans or promises. He will be going back to Australia for the summer to work in his father's business, and he plans to return in the fall, so they will write over the summer break, because they are great friends.

# Chapter 19

On Elizabeth's first day home for the summer, Mama lets her sleep until she wakes up on her own at nearly noon. Then she makes her way down the narrow hall from her cozy bedroom at the back of the house where she finds Mama with her Bible open, reading in Proverbs about the virtuous woman.

Questions about this passage have lurked in the back of Elizabeth's mind, so she decides to ask them. "Can any woman do all those things, or is the woman in Proverbs a composite? Is that perhaps why the passage begins with, 'Who can find a virtuous woman?' Can she really be found on this earth? Is she who we strive to be and only partially achieve?"

Mama admits that she does not know the answer to those questions, but she knows she finds plenty to emulate, and that works for her.

Elizabeth sees the section that people seem to quote most often from this passage, Verse 28, "Her children arise up, and call her blessed; her husband also, and he praiseth her." No wonder that verse is so often quoted, she thinks. What mother would not want that reward, that heritage, and that blessing to be hers?

However, Elizabeth, not yet a mother, finds that a different verse stands out to her. Verse 26 says, "She openeth her mouth with wisdom; and in her tongue is the law of kindness." She would like to make this her "life verse," but there are so many other favorites that have taken residence in her soul, such as Gal. 2:20 and Phil. 1:6 and Eph. 4:32 and Col. 2:6-7. Okay, she decides, she will make it one of her life verses.

"Mama," she asks, "What is your favorite verse?"

Mama answers by rattling off several, and one that made both their lists is Col. 2:6-7.

"It seems all-encompassing concerning our daily living," she says, then repeats it aloud. "As you have therefore received Christ Jesus the Lord, so walk ye in him: Rooted and built up in him and stablished in the faith, as ye have been taught, abounding therein with thanksgiving."

Mama and Elizabeth spend their summer as usual, putting up peaches and garden vegetables, decorating the house daily with fresh flowers, singing in the church choir, and talking.

This summer, Elizabeth once again does volunteer cleaning for her older friends. For Grandma, she and Jeannie do it together during her visits. Jeannie is now able to do so much, including spending many of her evenings in Erwin down at the softball field, watching and planning how she can be part of a team by the time another season rolls around. She is encouraged by the encouragers and undaunted by the discouragers. Elizabeth is one of her strongest encouragers, because she believes people should dream. Children dream, but so often their dreams are erased from their lives by well-meaning adults, who seem to wrongly view dreaming as the antithesis of responsibility. Elizabeth believes dreams help people learn how to recognize and experience the incredible possibilities opening up before them. She thinks dreams should be active until a person closes his or her eyes in death.

The summer also brings Phillip's return from England, beginning with a short visit at Aunt Jan's. He has a different air about him, seeming too subdued, and Elizabeth wonders if that is a good thing. There is also an elusiveness about him that she has never noticed before.

"What has happened to our comfortableness with each other?" she asks herself. "Does it have to do with his year abroad or with the seeming concern he hinted at about going home to Charleston?"

She focuses on the fact that in their years of being friends, he has never shared openly about his family in South Carolina. It is an intensely private part of his life. All she knows is his devotion to Aunt Jan.

Jeannie misses meeting Phillip by three hours. Still, she insists, without ever seeing his face, that he is the man for Elizabeth.

As Elizabeth packs for returning to campus, she has a little talk with herself, asking, "What will my last year of school bring? I must be discerning and only commit myself to what would be wise for me. I functioned so well in the flexibility of last year. Perhaps I should give myself that same kind of space again before the 'real world' grabs me."

# Chapter 20

Back on campus, Elizabeth delights in seeing Jeannie every day. She introduces her to Jen and Morgan, the two people who shared the most of Elizabeth's moments the previous year.

Jen and Elizabeth immediately pronounce it a perfect afternoon to enjoy the slight nip in the air and take a hike by the creek. Though Jen and Elizabeth had been in touch over the summer through email, Jen had chosen to wait and share in person some significant happenings from the summer. They sit on a big rock in the middle of the stream and no one says a word, which is different for them. Usually Jen emotes and Elizabeth listens. Today, they both listen. Then, they laugh.

Finally, Jen says, "Just before I arrived home at the end of last semester, two of the boys that I told you about, the ones who spread the viscous rumors about me, met with my parents and my pastor in the pastor's study at our church. They confessed to their entire smear campaign directed toward morally innocent young girls. Remember that I was their first victim, and, as it turned out, their only one. Once it got so out of hand, a couple of the boys had pangs of guilt, and said that they wanted out. Complications arose from that, because of the possibility of blackmailing the two of them over past questionable activities.

"They vacillated for months and finally decided that the life they were living, by trying to save their own necks, was worse than the consequences of coming clean. They were not as hard and tough as the other two, and decency prevailed with them. The police were eventually brought into the matter and were able to piece together some of their criminal acts. When their court date arrives in October, the evidence will be there explaining many illegal events that have puzzled the sheriff's office for a couple of years. I will not have to be there, as I have already given a deposition. In addition, though what they did to me was personally devastating, it is small in the eyes of the court compared to their other offenses."

"Thankfully, the righting of the wrong before the town will play itself out as clear. I will be legally declared vindicated from the malicious gossip. Of course, once a person's reputation has suffered a major blow, there will continue to be people who want to propagate the rumors, even after they have been unequivocally established as lies. Of course, there are those whose tongues are so turned toward the flesh, that they can change innocence into guilt with one conversation. Anyone can be a victim. Even as I guard my reputation, or my good name as it says in Proverbs, for the sake of my testimony and for the sake of my walk, I cannot guard the twisting of it.

"So, although I am vindicated in the eyes of my community, I will continue to be the target of individual gossip-mongers, whose job is to cast doubt on the vulnerable. I will not be their only target, nor will I probably ever again be their most prominent one, but I will have a place in their files for ready access when other gossip is slow. The book of James tells us about the power of the tongue. The saddest part of the untamed tongue is not that the unsaved are quick to use it for condemnation and ruin, but that the saved are highly skilled at it."

"Jen, what about your parents?" Elizabeth asks.

"They are broken with remorse that they ever questioned me, since I have been obedient and true to their guidelines throughout the years. My head forgives them, but my heart is clinging to the hurt, more concerning my mom than my dad. I once heard that hurt is anger in disguise. When I analyze that idea, I can see it. Surely, it is much more palatable to call an injustice hurt than to call it anger. People understand and sympathize with hurt, but they are put off by anger. A Christian can remain in his crippled state of hurt for a lifetime without being forced to deal with it, because he is seen as a victim, but if it is called anger, that puts it in a new light. As much as I want to walk well with the Lord, right now, I want to hang on to this hurt, this anger."

"Oh, Jen," Elizabeth says as she hugs her long and feels Jen's tears dampening her shoulder.

"It is Jen's mother who should be where I am now." Elizabeth tells herself.

Then Elizabeth explains to Jen something that she learned from Mrs. Sims in Erwin. "Probably the most sensitive and intense relationships, throughout the ages, exist between mothers and daughters. They are bound in the womb as kindred spirits. They understand each other seemingly too well, so they develop a way to hide from each other, as if that will gain them individuality and freedom. What it actually grants them is distance and confusion. Your mother is devastated over the breach she created between the two of you by distrusting you, her trustworthy girl. She is aching over the way she broke your heart. Her pain is for you. What will it take for her to deal with your stone-cold anger? Remember that Ephesians 4:32 says, 'Be ye kind to one another, tenderhearted, forgiving one another as God, for Christ's sake, hath forgiven you.' It is an act of gratitude on our part, to forgive because He forgave.

"Think about it, Jen. If you put those things on a balance, like the scales of justice, your mother's gross injustice would actually tip the scales. That is because it was and is unjust, and justice is the only criteria of the scale. Today, when God requires justice, He sees that it was settled by the cross. Today, God looks at us in light of Jesus' payment. He wants us to do, for every infraction, what He did for us eternally. He wants us to forgive all.

Elizabeth then pleads with Jen to go home with her for the weekend and spend some time with Mrs. Bach.

"Quite frankly," she says, "I am praying that you can settle this forgiveness in your heart today. Even so, you need Mrs. Bach for your future. And, how long do we have these ladies before the Lord takes them home?"

Jen agrees.

Elizabeth ponders why she chose Mrs. Bach for Jen to talk to. She knows nothing about her that would make her a better choice than the others. It just seems that her name naturally rolled off Elizabeth's tongue.

# Chapter 21

Mama is surprised to see them home on the first Saturday morning after classes have begun. She is glad though. She heads straight for the kitchen and makes a lemon icebox pie, while the girls jog over to Mrs. Bach's. They find her sitting in the double glider, under a towering oak, in her front yard, which is where she can be found most Saturday mornings, waving at all those passing by. Her blue eyes sparkle and her ruby red lips turn up in an instant, wide smile when she sees them. She pats the side of the glider facing her and invites them to sit with her. She would love to have them snuggled up beside her, but because of her hearing problem, they can converse better if she can see their not-so "ruby red" lips. They engage in lots of small talk before Elizabeth tells her about Jen's struggle. Mrs. Bach sends Elizabeth into the house to fix lemonade, and she listens attentively to Jen, while praying in her heart for direction in her response.

She says things similar to those Elizabeth had said to Jen a couple of days before. Those hours spent cleaning Mrs. Bach's house for several summers taught Elizabeth much more than a servant's heart. They taught her the beginnings of a woman's heart, one that promises to serve her well in the future.

When Elizabeth returns with the lemonade, Mrs. Bach is about to relate a story to Jen of grief and triumph from her own life. And she invites Elizabeth to stay.

"When I was a young woman, newly married, and living on an army base in Germany, I was alone a lot at night. One night, my husband's good friend dropped by to borrow a hammer and some nails. As I went to the closet to get them, I turned to find him too close for comfort. With a calm demeanor that betrayed my inner fear, I asked him to please leave, but suddenly he forced a kiss on me just when my next-door neighbor entered my unlocked door, as people often did back then. In that split second, she turned and left, with all her misinformation rapidly snowballing in her mind. Also, in that instant, my attacker was scared away by her brief presence. I had been spared a physical rape, but not an emotional one. News travels like wildfire on an army base, and my husband had heard the false, sordid, and embellished details before he returned home, following his shift, a little after midnight.

"He found me, his timid young bride, huddled in a locked bathroom, my eyes swollen almost shut from crying. When I realized it was he and felt safe to open the door, his expression told me that he knew, but that he did not know the truth. He refused to talk to me or to touch me. As far as he was concerned, I was, what was called in those days, 'damaged goods.' If only he had known that, although my heart was damaged, my body was still pure and whole. But he sent me home to my parents. He also asked for a divorce, but I refused to give him one. I had married "for better or for worse," and my marriage vows were sacred to me.

Back then, a person could not get a divorce at the drop of a hat. Laws protected marriage, and made it difficult to dissolve. With both those things working against his divorcing me, and because his refusal to believe the truth distorted his thinking, he began to drink heavily. One night, on the freeway, he swerved into the path of a Greyhound bus and was killed instantly. I wondered for many years how I would put it all behind me."

She pauses and continues, "I knew the Lord and I loved Him, but I had no intimacy in my relationship with Him. I did not know how to tap His strength for myself. I felt as if I were on a tedious climb out of a deep, dark hole, where I could see the flicker of light overhead, but I could not reach its full brilliance.

"My Aunt Ella, in Erwin, asked me to come and stay with her for a while, so we could help each other. It was very typical back then for families to move in and help each other. She was rearing her two young grandchildren, while their mother was recuperating from a long bout of tuberculosis. Aunt Ella had no time anymore to help Uncle Hugh in the shoe store. So I worked in the store Monday through Friday during the day, helped with the children in the evenings, and joined in Aunt Ella's Bible study to her neighbor ladies every Saturday morning. During that time, the Lord penetrated the deep recess of my heart, to heal it and to train it."

Mrs. Bach gives that last statement time to sink into her listeners' minds before continuing. "I enjoyed the constant flow of people in and out of the shoe store. It was the busiest and most fun in the fall, fitting youngsters with new school shoes.

"Because we were on the east side of the downtown square,

which looks today quite like it looked then, we got the morning sun. One of my jobs was to open the awnings for the day to a position that blocked the sun, but still allowed customers to window shop, then to close them at the end of the day. Soon, a young widower who dropped off his company's daily receipts every afternoon at the bank two doors away, made it part of his routine to help me with this small task. As winter approached, and he noticed that I walked home, he asked if he could drive me. I think you know the rest of the story. Hap and I married the next spring and I have been a fixture in Erwin ever since."

Though her story is finished, her advice is still forthcoming. "In summary, girls, remember that Christians are not exempt from hardship. Hardship breaks us. When we bring our brokenness to the Lord, He can make us more pliable than we were before, and use us in the healing of others."

Jen finally finds the missing piece of the puzzle while listening to Mrs. Bach. For her, it is purpose. She can now see that there is an eternal purpose in what she experienced, if she lets the Lord perfect it in her through total forgiveness. Jen asks Mrs. Bach if she will write to her as an encouragement, and Mrs. Bach agrees.

The girls head back to Mama's for some fried pork chops with mashed potatoes and gravy and a large slice of pie. Finally, they each take their turn in a relaxing tub bath, since a community shower is all they will see for the next few weeks.

# Chapter 22

Jen and Elizabeth, having left after church and a quick lunch on Sunday, get back to campus in time for that night's singspiration. As they arrive, who do they see strolling down the hill but Jeannie and Morgan. They already look like more than friends. Of course, they are, as Anne of Green Gables would express, "kindred spirits." Their sense of humor, unquenchable drive, and love of adventure are well defined and nearly identical.

Elizabeth's classes this semester prove to be more time-consuming than difficult. She has tried, since she had the mono, not to overload herself, which now means fewer trips home for a while. Perhaps, she thinks that is designed to be part of her weaning process from Mama. She doesn't know what next year will bring. Maybe she will be taken away from Erwin. Maybe she needs to see past her warm and encompassing little world.

Suzette is back. Mama had specifically asked Elizabeth to bring her for another visit, but Elizabeth has been remiss in following through. Since they are in one class together, Elizabeth asks Suzette about studying together for the mid-term exam. This puts them in close proximity and gives them more of a comfort level. Elizabeth expects Suzette is uneasy, wondering if Elizabeth figured out that she had taken Mama's necklace, then sneaked it into Elizabeth's jewelry case. Elizabeth also has to admit that she is a bit uneasy about taking Suzette again into her most cherished place, Mama's home. But she knows Mama is not uneasy at all. Rather, she is waiting for the opportunity to move a young girl from mediocrity to largess.

Both girls are out of class at noon on Fridays, so they pack the car right after breakfast, go to their class, then grab a sandwich from the cafeteria to eat on their way. They are on the road by 12:15, riding with all the windows down enjoying the wind blowing through their hair. It reminds Elizabeth of those old movies from the forties, except that she and Suzette are not wearing headscarves. She mentions this to Suzette and they laugh at the thought of it. They also laugh at how they inhaled their sandwiches. And they laugh at the dirt on their windshield. It is a laughing day, and Elizabeth is glad, as it quells any tensions. It also makes Suzette thankful that she agreed to go.

Mama knows they are coming and she is waiting impatiently, which is not characteristic of her. They arrive in time for a nap before supper, waking up to the aroma of fried pork chops. After eating, they sit on the swing and talk until they are chilled. Then it's time for hot chocolate by the fire. This cozy evening gives Elizabeth no hint of Mama's plan, but she is confident that Mama has one.

On Saturday, they pop out of bed at the sound of honking horns. A group of the youth from church has shown up to put up storm screens on Mama's windows. There are several groups, covering four other houses, doing whatever jobs need to be done to prepare for winter. Suzette is stunned to see their fun. It is the ideal time for Mama to share one of her favorite pieces of wisdom, that people become better friends working together than they do playing together. Elizabeth has often found that to be true in her life, as she peels bushel after bushel of peaches with Mama every summer, and cleans houses for her ladies in Erwin, who always pitch in and help.

Mama has chilidogs for everyone for lunch, then the crew is off to their afternoon shift. After the kitchen is cleaned up, Mama asks the girls to sit with her for a cup of tea. As they chat, Mama fingers the necklace around her neck and says, with the kindest voice, "This necklace was once lost, but now it is found."

Suzette's eyes well up with tears as she blurts out that the necklace was not lost, but rather it was stolen by her and then returned to Elizabeth's jewelry case when she thought she was going to get caught.

At that point, Mama removes the necklace from around her own neck and carefully places it around Suzette's, saying, "This necklace was once stolen, but now it is returned, by a young woman who has learned the value of truth."

Next Mama's hands slide around to cup Suzette's face and she kisses her forehead.

Suzette places her hands on Mama's hands, locks her eyes with Mama's eyes, and says, "Thanking you one thousand times will not be enough."

Mama smiles as she replies, "Thanking me once is sufficient, and you are welcome."

Mama believes that Suzette is not only relieved, but also is impacted for life. And she thinks that one cannot anticipate the unexpected things that will have a life-sized impact.

# Chapter 23

With the year in England behind him, Phillip is back at Emory, working on a master's degree in engineering. He writes more now, and seems to have regained his former contentment. Elizabeth is thrilled about that, and also glad he will be at Aunt Jan's for Thanksgiving. She plans ahead, and decides not to invite friends home with her this holiday, so she can dedicate herself to her and Phillip's friendship. Since they met once so long ago and again a couple of years ago, they have had mostly a long-distance friendship that is warm and kind and insightful. Still, she feels that Phillip knows her better than she knows him.

Jeannie will be in town at Grandma's with her entire family. It will be her time to finally meet the elusive Mr. Winn. Can Elizabeth keep her subdued?

Mama opts to accept one of their many invitations for Thanksgiving dinner. The plan is to go to Aunt Jan's, whose crowd is also scant this year. However, the menu will be full of the usual fare, including one of Elizabeth's favorites, Aunt Jan's cranberry congealed salad with oranges and pecans.

Phillip comes at noon to escort them over. His manners

are impeccable, and the two women feel like royalty. During the meal, they enjoy the British nuances Phillip has picked up over the last year. His comfort level with tea and the subtle and prolonged enjoyment of a cup with cream and a cube of sugar, is a pleasure for Elizabeth to watch. The meal and after-dinner talk pass too quickly. Phillip helps to clear the table, then, explaining that he needs one evening to unwind from his rigorous study schedule, politely excuses himself.

Mama and Elizabeth talk later, and Elizabeth senses that Mama knows some things about Phillip that she doesn't, which does not surprise her. She has learned better than to ask, because Mama tells what she wants to tell when she wants to tell it. Interestingly, her timing generally coincides with the time Elizabeth needs to hear it.

On Friday morning, Elizabeth shows up at Aunt Jan's front door in jeans, a flannel shirt, and hiking boots. She hopes it is an outfit that looks familiar to Phillip. It does, and it brings a sudden and infectious smile to his rested face. Aunt Jan quickly fixes turkey sandwiches for their outing, and they are off.

The warm day for this time of year is nice, as hiking through the woods, by the stream is more than a bit chilling on a cold day. Elizabeth enjoys the warmth in their conversation as well, as they sit in a nest of fallen leaves, munching their picnic fare.

Slowly, he clears his throat and says, "Elizabeth, in the years we have been friends, I have never told you about my mother."

After a slight pause, he begins. "We lived in England for two years when I was a toddler. Mom was stricken with weakness and a high fever on a holiday in Ireland, and it took Dad two days to get her from the country area, where we were camping, back to civilization and on to London and her own doctor. When the doctor saw her, he immediately admitted her to the hospital. She had meningitis. The prognosis boiled down to two things, brain damage or death. Dad hired a nanny to take care of me, while he spent almost every off-duty minute at the hospital. In the several months before Mom could travel, Dad exhausted himself and went into a deep depression. The military had to send them both back to the U.S. as patients, and then gave Dad a medical discharge. Our nanny made the trip back with us to take care of me, staying for several weeks, until everyone was acclimated and in somewhat of a routine."

Elizabeth nods, caught up in the story.

"Dad eventually recovered well in his familiar surroundings and with family support, especially from Aunt Jan, who visited regularly and often took me back home with her from one visit till the next."

Phillip hesitates, then continues.

"Mom never recovered and is still living today in a state home, where her condition demands care around the clock. Dad has a twenty-two year history of visiting her three nights a week and every Sunday, for the entire day. He has been dutiful and tender and true. Those are great attributes that have instilled themselves deep in me. Yet, he has never been able to show me the excitement of a typical husband-wife relationship. He also has not been able to draw me into a typical father-son relationship, because his emotions have been wrapped up, and used up, in his care of Mom. I never resented that, as I had extended family who filled the gaps. Again, it was Aunt Jan who related to me the most and the best. Now, you can see the reason for my devotion to her."

Again, Elizabeth quietly nods.

"While finishing my senior year at Emory and preparing for my year of studies in England, I made it a goal to find my former nanny and reconnect with her during my stay. I ran into a lot of roadblocks during my long-distance search. Dad helped all he could with names of people and places, but I traveled down one dead end after another. I decided that an in-person search would be more profitable and provide diversion from the books once I was settled there.

In making friends with locals, I surprisingly met a young woman at a reading at the library, who thought she could point me in the right direction. Soon, she introduced me to her friend, who took me to meet her mother. I carried in my billfold the one picture that shows well the facial features of my nanny and me, when her face was young and smooth, and mine was chubby and childlike. As I placed it before her, she cried. She told me that she had written for a few years, but the letters gave way to only Christmas cards and then to nothing, as her own life became complicated. She regretted losing touch and was overwhelmed at seeing me. Her daughter, Opal, is several years younger than I am, and was just beginning the university. She is bright and beautiful, and we developed a closeness. For me it was kinship, but for her it was romance."

Elizabeth realizes she now has an explanation for the friendly picture.

"As time passed," Phillip continues, "Opal increasingly infiltrated my life, taking over my time. I began to feel smothered. I learned that she was following me, and checking with friends about me. I was at the mercy of a woman who seemed to be inching herself into every area of my life, and who somehow knew too much. It was oppressive. I was an ocean away from everyone I knew well and trusted. I had no one to talk to. I wanted to return home, but I had a job to finish. I tried to distance myself from Opal, which only proved to escalate her quest and improve her mind games. I felt my own steadiness slipping in the same place that my mother lost her health, and my dad lost his dream."

Elizabeth feels a tear about to spill over.

"I have not talked to anyone about this, Elizabeth, till now. I needed to tell someone with a sensitive heart who would understand and not judge. I needed to share it as a way of finally setting it to rest, but I did not want to exploit Opal, nor did I want to reinforce the event by cementing it in the minds of others, who could keep its shadowy side alive. Thank you for being my safe sounding board. And thank you, Elizabeth, because I know without even asking that you will pray for Opal."

With that said, Phillip's mood changes to playfulness. He scoops Elizabeth up in his strong arms and turns in circles as the sun catches their faces through the bare branches of the trees. Their eyes meet, and she senses Phillip is going to kiss her. It is a breathtaking moment of anticipation that transforms itself into the encompassing suspension of all the love one kiss can express. They laugh and throw leaves at each other and hug and laugh some more.

The hike back is a new road, not literally, but figuratively. It is a road of hopes and dreams that pulsates in their hearts, while at the same time spreading calmness through their minds.

Their faces betray the coolness they had planned to exhibit as they return to Mama's kitchen where she and Aunt Jan are sharing a pot of tea. Though they try, they cannot deny this love revealed, and how its intensity took them both by surprise. A steady and deep friendship is indeed an ideal beginning for building an abiding and vibrant love.

They sit and pour themselves some tea before joining the ladies in examining old photos of past Christmases. Mama expresses her wishes to decorate the outside of the house this year, the way she did when Papa was alive. Phillip and Elizabeth are quick to volunteer their help. The four of them sort through the pictures, picking bits and pieces from several years to make up this year's design.

Mama can wait no longer to inquire, in her typical straight forward way, about the fact that the two of them cannot stop smiling, and that their gazes into each other's eyes seem unduly long and somewhat intimate. Aunt Jan smiles at Mama's question, and at what she has long believed in her heart would someday become reality.

Phillip begins, "You know that in our early years of seeing each other on holidays, I was mostly interested in playing ball with the boys in that vacant lot by David's house. I knew Elizabeth was over here, but we did not connect until that day her father went to the hospital, and she stayed with us at your house, Aunt Jan."

He smiles warmly and continues. "I flashed back to the time a year before, when my mom's condition began to deteriorate, and everyone in the family took turns staying with her at the hospital before she stabilized, returning our lives to the normalcy of being abnormal. It was scary for a young boy, but it was a growing time. From that day forward, my sensitive side has been acutely aware of the pain and uncertainty of others. It had its first real test with Elizabeth that night when she was eight and I was eleven. I was drawn to comforting her. It was the comfort of a boy, but it had, in some small way, the depth of a man who had grown deep by suffering.

"I wanted to protect her, because I remembered my own vulnerable feelings. But it was not my job to protect her, only to befriend her and comfort her. It would seem that a solid friendship would develop, but that was thwarted by Elizabeth's being lost to us for a decade. Still, I remembered her. I remembered her with every downturn of my mom's condition, with every Christmas program I attended with Aunt Jan, and with every hurt I saw in another. Elizabeth and I were loosely bound by that one night.

"When she came into my life again, I instantly knew our friendship would be solid. I was comfortable that we could come and go through each other's lives without losing each other again. I knew that we would continually be part of each other's Erwin experience, and I liked that. I had girlfriends, and I had Elizabeth, my anytime friend. More and more, the Lord impressed me with friendship as the absolutely most fertile ground for the growth of love. More and more, the picture of Elizabeth filled my mind. More and more, I wondered if my picture held a prominent place in the tender recesses of her mind."

After pausing to take a breath, Phillip resumes. "I determined that this Thanksgiving was the time to find out, but I was so nervous that I almost let the opportunity slip through my fingers.

When Elizabeth showed up today, wearing her hiking clothes, I knew that we must hike to my favorite spot, in hopes that it would also become hers. When she looked so naturally perky, with no makeup and that cute ponytail halfway hiding under her ball cap, I knew it was going to be a comfortable day. When she flashed her amazing smile, I knew I could muster the courage to learn what I had to know."

Elizabeth can wait no longer, and bursts out with, "We are in love."

Everyone laughs.

Phillip wants to celebrate the excitement of the day by taking the three of them to dinner tonight. He excuses himself, as he has some errands to run and a reservation to make. The women continue to drink tea and smile. Aunt Jan smiles the most because, as she declares, she has known for the longest.

Arriving at their table, Phillip, in his well-defined and gentlemanly way, seats each one in her proper place, by the specific rose and thank-you note he has set up for each. Mama and Aunt Jan have identical mussie-tussies of pink roses, but each has a different and well-thought-out note.

Aunt Jan reads hers aloud. " You have been my steady rudder on a small ship on choppy water. You have believed in me and guided me to be the gentleman who could attract and cherish Elizabeth. The deep pink roses are for gratitude and appreciation. Much love, Phillip"

Mama reads hers silently and a tear rolls down her cheek. Aunt Jan and Elizabeth want to know what it says, so Mama paraphrases. " It says that a very grateful young man loves the granddaughter whom I have helped to mold and point to the Lord."

Elizabeth's is a long-stem, red rose in a lovely crystal vase. The card says, "I love you, plain and simple, yet deep and committed."

"Who wants to eat?" Elizabeth speaks her thoughts. "We want to savor this moment till we have tasted each morsel of its significance."

She wishes for a camera to record these tender moments, only to find out that a waiter, who will get a very hefty tip, is capturing it all on video.

Elizabeth ponders the scene in her heart and wonders if it can get any better.

# Chapter 24

Later in the evening, Elizabeth fills Phillip in about Jeannie, whom he has heard of, but never met. He certainly never knew of her unrelenting prediction of their inevitable love match. While plans for introducing the two of them are formulating in Elizabeth's and Phillip's minds, the phone rings, and they hear Mama say, "Yes, Jeannie, Elizabeth is here. Just one minute."

"Hello, friend," Elizabeth says playfully.

Jeannie responds with mischief in her voice, "What are you so chipper about? Have you been seeing your very good friend, Phillip?"

Elizabeth tells her that she had Thanksgiving dinner with him at Aunt Jan's house.

With disappointment in her voice, Jeannie asks, "Is that all?"

Elizabeth quickly steers the conversation a bit and tells Jeannie that she will arrange for her to meet Phillip tomorrow if he is not busy. " I will call you back in a few minutes, okay?"

"Okay," she replies. "But, hurry!"

The plans are made for 8:00 A.M. Phillip wanders back home across the two yards and Elizabeth settles in for the night, drifting off into a deep and satisfying sleep.

The smell of pancakes wafts into Elizabeth's room as she wakes, stretches, and sets her mind to replaying yesterday's picnic for at least the one-hundredth time. Quickly, she dresses for the early morning event that she and Phillip have planned for Jeannie. They are to drive out to Uncle Jimmy's farm to scout for three Christmas trees this year, one for Mama, one for Aunt Jan, and one for Grandma. But they don't plan to chop them early this year because, as Mama can attest to from last year, it is truly difficult to keep them pretty and safe for a month.

From the instant Elizabeth and Phillip pick her up, Jeannie carefully watches them throughout the entire ride, searching for hints that something is going on. However, today, they are the picture of aloofness and casual friendship, which is the first phase of their well-designed plan.

As they are about to decide on a tree for Aunt Jan, Phillip relates, almost matter-of-factly, that he will not be available for the chopping, transporting, and setting up of the trees, as he has been spending a lot of time with a girl at school who has become more than just another date. He thinks there may be something developing. She wants to take him home with her to spend most of the break meeting and getting to know her family.

The unconcealed panic on Jeannie's face shows that their plan is working. Elizabeth and Phillip both notice her intense reaction. But Phillip pretends to not notice, while Elizabeth looks at Jeannie with piercing eyes and a slight shaking of her head, implying that she needs to shape up.

Jeannie's return look to Elizabeth is disbelief and shock that

Phillip has another girlfriend. She wonders how she could have been so wrong, and how Elizabeth cannot see that he is the one for her and he is getting away.

Jeannie loses interest in looking for trees, so Elizabeth finds one for Grandma that will fit her living room picture window perfectly, as it is not too tall, but is wide and full. They tag it with a piece of orange ribbon and continue the hunt for Mama's tree.

On the ride back, they stop at a little roadside cider stand and soothe their chilled bodies with the steaming hot, cinnamon-topped treat. Jeannie leans forward from the back seat and curtly asks Phillip to explain what is so great about this girl he is dating. Had Phillip not been forewarned about Jeannie's long-standing conviction about him and Elizabeth, he would probably wonder at her sanity. However, since he knows, he continues to draw her into this game by explaining that the thing he enjoys most about his girlfriend is her free spirit. He likes it that she feels good enough about herself to wear her hair in a bit of a punk style, and he enjoys that she talks loud, often calling attention to herself in a funny sort of way.

"She is so comfortable in her skin," he explains, "that being with her causes me to stretch my own personality."

Jeannie says, "But that is so different from Eliz.... uh, I mean, so different from the kind of girl I thought you would like, by the way Elizabeth described you to me."

"Well," replies Phillip, speaking slowly to peak Jeannie's interest even more, "I like different kinds of girls. I really like Elizabeth for a true-blue friend. I think anyone would."

He winks flirtatiously at Elizabeth, leading Jeannie to think he is also a two-timer.

Jeannie is appalled that she has wasted so much time and energy picturing Phillip as Elizabeth's ideal man. She wonders why Elizabeth has remained his friend through the years, when he is seemingly so shallow. Elizabeth had even told her that he was sensitive and deep. How could Elizabeth have been so unobservant, Jeannie wonders, thinking this is a bad dream and wanting to wake up?

They stop on the way home, at Walgreen's, where Phillip runs in to pick up some photos. He opens the package and looks at them, smiling as he saunters to the car. He tucks the photos into the visor and heads toward Mama's house, where she has put the restaurant video in, as Phillip's requested when he called her from inside the drugstore.

Jeannie would rather go back to Grandma's house, as she is disgusted, but Elizabeth begs her to come in because Mama is looking forward to seeing her. "She really wants to see you walk up the front steps," Elizabeth explains.

When they walk into the den, Mama begins the video taken the evening before and a voice announces, "A Night of Gratitude and Love." Jeannie thinks it is a movie and pays very little attention until she hears Elizabeth gasp with awe. She looks at Elizabeth and suddenly realizes that the gasp is coming from a video playing on the television. It only takes a moment for her to realize that she has been duped by two of the best. She excitedly watches and absorbs each amazing detail. She cries that it has finally happened, she laughs that it is a joyful time, and she declares revenge for their dastardly deed of tricking her.

# Chapter 25

Back on campus, all are studying for exams, and many are edgy from lack of sleep. The post office is a busy place, with all the care packages from mothers who want to spur on their college kids to make those A's.

Morgan brings Jeannie's package to her dorm, since it is too big for her to carry and balance well even though, on an ordinary day, few would know that Jeannie has a prosthesis. She has mastered regular walking and simple stairs with a rail. She is working on a fast-paced walk, with her therapists in Atlanta once a week. The trip there and back has been hard, as she has been hiring a cab throughout the semester. However, Morgan, who wants to see her gain complete use of her prosthesis, has committed to taking her if she can change her appointment time to fit with his schedule. She jumps at the chance, as she finds his company exhilarating. She laughs more with him than she does with all her other friends combined.

Since Jeannie does not answer a page, Morgan leaves the package in the lobby. When she arrives and finds it too heavy to drag to her room, she opens it right where it is. It is a new sewing machine that her parents purchased for the resident assistant in Jeannie's dorm. She has been a jewel to Jeannie and to them. It is a small thing to them, but will be a very big thing to the R.A., as she makes extra money from doing sewing and mending for students. The Greenes noticed that her old machine had become a source of frustration and expense for her. Since they wanted it to be anonymous, they had sent it to Jeannie with a letter stating their wish. Now it is open in the lobby.

Jeannie makes her way to her room to hide the letter and returns with a big red bow and a sign that says, "To Sue."

Thankfully, no one is around to see this little episode except Mary, who was at the desk in the lobby when Morgan delivered the package and has now been included in the secret. The only other person Jeannie must caution is Morgan to keep the secret safe.

By the time everyone finishes dinner and returns to the dorm, Sue has not only discovered the machine, but has already set it up in the place of her worn-out one. She has skipped dinner and opted for a peanut butter and jelly sandwich in her apartment, since she could not wait to check out all the bells and whistles on this new, and so welcomed, gift.

At eight, Sue announces over the intercom for all the girls to come to her apartment for a surprise. Of course, they are expecting cookies, since Sue always shares her care packages from her grandmother, who has learned to send enough goodies for fifty. Though their taste buds were already primed, they are far more excited to share Sue's excitement over the mysterious gift. It is Christmas come early, which reminds the girls that they need to escalate their efforts for the upcoming and highly competitive decorating contest among all the dorms.

The girls have been making their plans all year, but the time has slipped up on everyone except Kim and the ones she has corralled during the last week to check the strings of lights for burned-out bulbs. While they are assembled this time, they divide up their jobs and make plans to do the actual decorating on Saturday morning.

When the workday arrives, Morgan strolls by and finds Jeannie on the second rung of a ladder, attempting to climb higher so she can hang lights on a window. He knows she is difficult to contain, and his own adventurous spirit identifies with hers, but he feels his heart race. He cannot get to her fast enough. Just as he can reach out and touch her, she slips, and her fall is broken by his strong arms and steady stance. Fortunately, she is only bruised on her "natural born leg" as she likes to call it. She will be hobbling for the last few weeks of the semester. Morgan hopes it is enough of an inconvenience to make her think twice before pulling another such precarious stunt.

Jeannie's trips to therapy have been especially fruitful and her drives with Morgan have been happily intense. Since they cannot compete yet physically, they compete mentally. Their fun-loving personalities keep them laughing uproariously at each other and themselves. However, this sudden trip to the doctor is not so much fun, as Jeannie struggles to find a comfortable position in the midst of the pain and escalating soreness from the fall. Upon examination, they find that a piece of her prosthesis is loose and would have eventually become more uncomfortable if it had not been found and repaired. Jeannie deems the fall providential and smiles. Morgan loves her smile. He loves so much about Jeannie, but he is not ready to be "in love."

Jeannie's instructions are to rest, in order to be ready for Saturday's events, and she reluctantly agrees. Waiting is difficult, but time marches on, and Saturday finally arrives. Thinking she is up alone, she soon finds that there is no sleeping in for anyone. Kim is calling on the intercom at five-minute intervals until every girl is standing in front of her. Being an early riser, Kim jokingly calls the stragglers sluggards. They agree, but tell her that their social life is much more thrilling than hers, which brings a hearty chorus of friendly laughter.

They delve excitedly into their tasks. Morgan comes to check on Jeannie, who is being watched like a hawk by Elizabeth, especially, and by the rest of her dorm mates as well. Jeannie has been given the little-sought-after job of unwrapping the ornaments and glass balls for the tree. And, because she regards any job that includes her in the action as good, she does it with finesse. At the bottom of the box, stuck slightly under a section of cardboard and looking as if it had just slid out of a long time hiding place, she finds a pendant from a necklace. Before examining it, she calls Sue over, since she is a senior and would have a three-year history with this box.

"Do you recognize this or remember anyone losing it last year?" she asks.

Sue carefully studies it, noticing that the link for attaching it to the necklace is twisted. She turns over the dainty gold heart with a small diamond in the center and sees the inscription on the back. She realizes that getting this heart back to its owner is imperative and urgent.

Sue tells Jeannie that the box had been donated to the girls when she was a freshman, by another freshman, Stacey, who had dropped out of school after the fall semester to care for her mother, whose body was riddled with cancer.

"I kept up with Stacey for a while," Sue says. "But then we lost touch. I will check on Monday with the business office, to see if they have an address for her."

Jeannie relishes a good mystery and lets her mind explore several possibilities, but none equal the true story that is soon to unfold.

The decorating is done in time to assess it and fine-tune things before the contest on the following Friday. Kim is the most pleased of anyone, with her favorite part being the life-size story of Jesus on the lawn out front. She reminded the girls from the onset of this project that Jesus' birthday is what is celebrated at Christmas, but that she wanted to carry the theme all the way through the cross, the empty tomb, and the ascension. She said she wanted to give every Christian a reminder that Christ has done it all for us, and give all non-Christians a clear picture of the peace, security, and glory that can be theirs in Christ.

The business office door is barely unlocked, when Sue walks in asking to get an appointment with the registrar. She is not available until 4:30, and Sue quickly accepts the appointment.

Sue asks Elizabeth to go to the appointment with her, and they arrive thirty minutes early. Though they want to get the pendant back to its rightful owner, they are especially interested in the long-ago date on the inscription, and know it must have immense sentimental value.

When asked if she remembers Stacey Wright, Mrs. Hamilton's expression becomes quizzical, as she wonders why these young women would ask about her on this particular day.

She answers, "This morning's mail brought an application from Stacey to return to school, along with a lengthy letter recounting her last three years. She had nursed her mother through chemotherapy and radiation at their local hospital, after which her mother was accepted into an experimental program at Johns Hopkins. Stacey spent the next two years going back and forth from Richmond to Baltimore, accompanying her mother for treatments, which seemed to be working only minimally, as improvements seemed small. At the end of those two years, however, the hair she had lost was growing back and her energy was slowly returning. After another year, she had gained enough strength to do much for herself and her family. With her prognosis much improved, she insisted that Stacey go back to school. Stacey's desire is to begin in January, and we will certainly do our best to make that happen."

She continues, "Now. Would you like to share your sudden interest in Stacey with me?"

Sue shows the inscribed heart to Mrs. Hamilton, and says, "We found a pendant that seemed to have been hiding for perhaps a very long time in the crevice of a box of Christmas decorations, which Stacey gave us just before she left school three years ago. As you examine it, you can see our urgency to find its rightful owner."

Mrs. Hamilton gazes at the inscription at length, nods her head in agreement, and gives Stacey's phone number to her friend, Sue.

The girls call Stacey immediately, to ask if the pendant they are holding is familiar to her. Stacey bursts into a combination of laughter and sobs as she begs them to hold the line for a minute. She takes the extension phone to her mother and asks the girls to tell both of them the complete story of how it came to be in their possession. Stacey and her mother listen, with rapt attention, savoring every detail of how the heart was preserved in such an unlikely place, and undisturbed for so long.

It is now their turn to give the background on this unusual find. Stacey asks her mother to share the story, since she knows it best, and because Stacey never tires of hearing it.

Mrs. Wright begins with vibrancy in her voice that betrays the tiredness she feels on this particular day, in which she has attempted to do too much simply to prove to her husband and Stacey that she can.

Warmly, she begins, "When Dad was coming home from WWII after a tour in the Pacific, he sent several personal things ahead with specific instructions that the boxes not be opened until he arrived. On the long voyage home, he died mysteriously aboard ship. The military personnel was never able to give my mother a clear answer as to what happened, but one thing was clear, our family would never be the same. Mom did not have a husband, and I did not have a father.

"After the body was sent home, we staunchly made our way through the funeral and burial, and tried to settle into a routine again. At that point, Mom knew it was time to open the boxes her beloved Charlie had sent home. She included me, as I was seven then, and she knew that though my memories of Dad were obviously not nearly as developed as hers, I remembered him well and loved him so."

Mrs. Wright takes a moment to reflect on this memory before continuing. "We held up the silk pillows from the islands and decided they belonged on Mom's bed as a constant reminder that Dad had picked them out for her. Those few snapshots included in the boxes became treasured possessions. The remainder was rather nondescript, except for a small gift-wrapped box, packaged securely and cushioned by some tissue paper. I remember distinctly how Mom slowly opened it, dreaming about Dad as she removed each piece of tape to somehow make him seem closer. I learned an important lesson that day, that memories do make a person seem close again. As young as I was, I determined to make good memories to draw from when I would need them."

There is another pause and the girls want to fill the silence, but they don't dare. They wait and soon, Mrs. Wright once more continues. "When the lid was open and the cotton removed from the top of the box, it revealed what Mom described as 'the loveliest necklace in the world' with an inscription, 'Love, Charlie 1945.'

"I readily agreed, and helped her put it on. She then reached down to close the box and noticed there was a paper underneath the bottom layer of cotton. Her hands toyed with lifting the cotton to retrieve the paper. She later told me that she thought it might be a bill of sale, and she did not think that Dad would want her to know how much he paid for this precious gift.

"Finally, she determined that if it were a receipt, she would simply put it in the safety deposit box at the bank and never look at it. Slowly, she picked it up, finding that it was a love note. She read it silently, and then she shared it with me as tears rolled down her cheeks and her voice became weaker and weaker. Though I was only a small girl, I read that note often with Mom, and committed it to memory, hoping that someday I would marry a man who loved me like Dad loved Mom. The note said, 'A small token of my great love for you, sweetheart. It represents every tender gaze, every passionate kiss, and every warm memory. As I write this, I envision myself fastening it around your neck and leaning forward to nibble your ear, my beloved and best friend. OXOXOXOX Charlie'"

There is a catch in Mrs. Wright's voice. She clears her throat and quickly proceeds. "Mom was a strong and determined lady who carried on with life. She reared me with the support of family and friends, and we never lacked for anything, as our desires were simple. Mom was content, even happy, though the tears would consistently be seen moistening her eyes on holidays, and especially on the anniversary of their wedding. She never had another romantic interest."

Stacey jumps into the conversation and guides her mother toward the recounting of how the necklace became hers.

As Mrs. Wright speaks again, tenderness is evident in her voice. "Mom had often promised that the necklace would one day be mine. On the evening that Neal came to ask my mom about marrying me, she was obviously ready for that moment, with her speech prepared. She said to Neal, 'Since you have been a part of this community and our church for your entire life, I have not only had the chance to watch you, but in some ways to help mold you. What a privilege it was for me as your fourth-grade Sunday School teacher to hear you answer Bible questions correctly, but it was much more of a privilege to watch you live out God's directives and principles as I observed your willingness to stand for Christ, sometimes standing alone in the midst of much peer pressure. If I could have handpicked the man to be my daughter's husband, the man to guard and cherish her heart, it would always have been you. I know in the depths of my soul that Charlie would have been saying the male version of what I am telling you now, if he were here. I can confidently give our blessing to you both as you prepare to live out your lives as one.

"Neal stood speechless. Then, after a brief pause, Mom said, 'I have long anticipated this day and made some preparations of my own. She handed the necklace in its original box to Neal with instructions not to open it until he was ready to place it around my neck at the rehearsal dinner on the eve of our wedding. I thought that was an unusual request, but reflecting on Mom's history of giving distinct purpose to everything, I did not question. I only smiled at the thought of wearing this symbol of romance and love.

"The most romantic part of all," she continues, "was when Neal opened the box to find a note on top that said, 'Read the back of the pendant together with joy before fastening it around Julia's neck.' Where it had read, 'Love, Charlie, 1945,' it now had an addition that read, 'Love, Neal, 1963.'"

Continuing on, she said, "Mom, however, was not the only clever romantic. Neal, having often heard the original note that Dad had sent to Mom, with perfect timing and flair, fastened the necklace around my neck and leaned forward to nibble my ear. Embarrassment overtook this young bride-to-be at that moment, but each replay only becomes more precious."

Stacey adds to the story, which continues with a mixture of

sadness and resolve. "Mom realized one evening as she was getting ready for bed and reached to remove the necklace, that the chain was broken and had fallen into her inner clothing, but the pendant was gone. She searched all her clothing carefully, with no success. Panic struck her!

"Where had she been and what had she done since morning when she put it on? She retraced her steps in her mind the next day, and we all physically retraced her steps. The search was organized and thorough, yet it turned up nothing. Mom knew, as sad as losing the pendant was, it could never compare to her mother losing her father. She took a deep breath and thanked the Lord for the purpose the pendant had served in her life, and for the abundance of memories connected to it that will not be lost. Still, she lamented and we cried together that the wearing of it would be lost to me. But she still could only be grateful for it's existence during two generations in her family and it's heritage as long as future generations keep its message of love alive."

Because the Wrights don't want to risk losing the pendant again, they ponder briefly how to get it back. Suddenly, Mr. Wright suggests that a trip for the entire family to the campus this weekend would be a special use of his frequent-flyer miles.

Sue and Elizabeth burst into laughter at the exact moment, realizing that the dorm-decorating contest is this weekend. What could be a more ideal setting for returning the pendant that was found in those specific decorations?

# Chapter 26

Friday arrives with fanfare. Like the little mice in the Cinderella story, the girls scurry to put last-minute details in place and set up their refreshment table with real linens and family crystal and silver platters brought from their homes after the Thanksgiving break. They take the last of their budgeted money to buy Christmas flowers, which Elizabeth and Jeannie arrange and place in highly visible areas of the lobby. Their extravaganza boasts deep red poinsettia blossoms and varying sizes of cut-glass ornaments to pick up the light, set succinctly in a trail of asparagus fern and baby's breath, beginning at one end of the serving table and ending at the other, sometimes weaving out and around the platters for a complete look of perfection. Replenishing the hot h'ors d'oevres will keep the girls busy, but the ready assortment of cheese balls and cookies, as well as Elizabeth's personal favorite, homemade cream puffs, will keep everyone's taste buds satiated, in case they are forced to wait a bit on the bubbling crab dip or sausage balls, piping hot from the oven.

Phillip arrives barely in time for the judging and just ahead of the Wrights, who have rented a car at the Atlanta airport. Elizabeth expects they passed each other back and forth along the highway.

Since he has heard the Wright family story, including Elizabeth's feelings connected to it, Phillip helps to calm her jitters at the excitement of this evening.

She appears composed as the judges wander through the outdoor scenes and open the door to enter the lobby of the dorm. At that instant, Sue catches a glimpse of Stacey and her parents rushing across the campus to be part of the action already taking place. Sue grabs Elizabeth's hand, and the two girls momentarily forget about the contest into which they have poured themselves, as a different scene is about to unfold. Sue and Elizabeth run through the crowd to welcome them. They embrace because, though only Sue knows Stacey, the family has become dear to them all in the excitement and the anticipation of this meeting.

Immediately, the Wrights assure Sue and Elizabeth that they want to save the pendant until the end of the festivities. The girls take a couple of deep breaths and refocus on the God-honoring scene, which they think is the best scene on the campus and know is a winner, whether it wins a blue ribbon or not, because it has the makings of winning lives for eternity.

The crowd follows the judges from dorm to dorm. As the judges survey their display, the girls search the faces of each for a hint of reaction, but all their opinions are simply recorded on their score sheets. The plan is to bring the ribbons to the dorms as the parties take place inside.

At Jackson Hall, there is piano music and carol singing, intermingled with skits, and, of course, the food. Each girl is scheduled to see other dorms, while taking turns covering her own.

Upon returning, the girls, find a red ribbon on their door. Sue and Elizabeth smile, thankful for any ribbon, and remember the confirmation in their spirits that they will only know when they see their Savior face to face how much of a blue-ribbon scene theirs truly is.

The partying continues until midnight, but Elizabeth excuses herself by 10:30, to go with the Wrights to Sue's apartment, where Sue serves hot chocolate, as if they need something more in their bloated stomachs.

Not wanting to delay the much-anticipated event any longer, Sue goes promptly, to her antique desk that, because of its own sentimental value, is an ideal temporary home for the pendant. Unlocking the top drawer just below the roll top and taking out a tiny, blue velvet drawstring bag, Sue realizes that she does not know into whose hands she should place the long-awaited treasure, as it is intricately interwoven into the hearts of Mrs. Wright, Mr. Wright, and Stacey. She had not expected this sudden questioning, but the answer comes to her quietly, much like the fog drifts in, "on little cat feet," in Carl Sandburg's poem, "The Fog." The pendant presently belongs to Mrs. Wright, no matter who possessed it in the past or who will possess it in the future.

Sue places the soft bag into the hands of Mrs. Wright, who gently opens it and reaches in to explore the cold metal, changed forever by its warm message. She hesitates before slipping it out, as she wants to savor the moment, assigning it a magnitude of its own. The scene seems to be suspended in time. When she slowly removes the heart from its soft, safe, temporary home, Mr. Wright, who is as prepared as his second mom, the one who had passed the pendant on to him to give to his beloved on the eve of their wedding, takes a gold chain from his pocket and the heart from his wife. All eyes are riveted on him as he attaches the heart to the chain, stands, and extends his hand to his wife to join him in the middle of the much smaller and more intimate group than the first time he enacted this scene. He fastens the necklace around her neck and leans forward to nibble her ear, to a mixture of cheers and tears.

Jeannie, who has just finished her final shift at the food table and who has never been shy, knocks on the door and asks if she may be part of the celebration, which she clearly heard into the lobby. When told that she surely may, she then asks about Morgan, who, of course, is also invited to revel in the latest chapter of this story of lost and found.

Can they maintain this euphoria through exam week?

# Chapter 27

Exams begin on Monday, so Phillip stays only long enough to help with clean up and heads back to Atlanta, hoping to get a little sleep before he begins his own cramming session. Elizabeth and Phillip will not see each other over the break, since he has committed to working with his uncle in Macon through the holidays, to make extra money. Saying Elizabeth will miss him is an understatement. Mama will also miss him, as will Aunt Jan, but Mama suspects the extra money has a specific purpose and she is pleased by her suspicions.

On Christmas Eve, Phillip surprises them by arriving at noon, because Uncle Nick said no one should work on Christmas Eve or Christmas, or the next day if it is a Sunday. Phillip has two entire days in Erwin, which he and Elizabeth fill to overflowing. He regrets that he was not here to chop and haul and set up the three Christmas trees, but he had previously asked Uncle Jimmy to arrange for all that to be done. Phillip now sees their lights twinkling in the living room windows of both houses in the middle of the day as he turns into Aunt Jan's driveway.

The Christmas Eve service at church is solemn, and it speaks to Elizabeth's mind as well as her heart, causing her to realize that as she graduates, she needs a plan. She has never had a long-term plan but to follow the Lord, and, so far, that has played itself out well. Yet, it seems to her that a young adult woman cannot continue without a job, even though there is money. But why not, if her life is useful? She will follow Mama's example, to do whatever is next.

Elizabeth and Phillip spend Christmas day and Sunday mostly with family, soaking up the quiet time together before another demanding semester.

As this final semester flies by much too rapidly for Elizabeth, she laments the upcoming time that she must leave the friends who have taken root in the fertile soil of her life and decides to escalate her investments in their lives. So she sets out to build more memories, knowing that memories are powerful and no one can build too many good ones.

Jeannie and she expect to be friends and unceasing soul mates from now through eternity. But they are realistic enough to know that after college, their lives may take them to different parts of the world or, at the very least, to different involvements that usurp their time, so they will cherish the range of experience and base of connection they have, and utilize creative ways to keep their relationship lively. They want to be more than Christmas card buddies a few years from now. Elizabeth spends time with Jeannie and Morgan together, as a way to be part of their bank of investments in each other.

On weekends, they take short hikes, since spring has arrived, and Jeannie is so proficient with her prosthesis. Only once did Morgan have to rescue her, carrying her over a mile of rugged terrain back to the car, after she slipped on a root while clowning for a picture.

Elizabeth thinks that Jeannie's exuberance about all of life is probably what attracts her most to her friend and probably what attracts Morgan as well.

Stacey and Sue resume their former friendship with an array of added dimensions. They find that they both enjoy the simple and sentimental things in life. Each has found a boyfriend. Sue's is a graduate from four years ago, but they only met when he moved back to the vicinity, taking a position in a small law office run by a friend of his father. The connection may have gotten him the job, but his tenacity and thoroughness make him the vital employee he has become. Elizabeth watches as he delights in pleasing Sue, and she flourishes in responding to his attentiveness. Elizabeth makes it her business to be in Sue's presence often, soaking up her sweet trust as an example for times when hers may again falter. She continues making memories that, she feels certain, will come to her rescue many times in the future.

Stacey and her boyfriend seem to be casual friends who enjoy similar things, and it works for now. He is a senior and has no idea about the direction of his life for the coming year. He has sent out many resumes and is now playing the waiting game. Stacey, though she is his age, still has most of her college career in front of her, and she is content with the status quo.

Care packages come weekly to Sue and Elizabeth from Stacey's parents, as their way of showing ongoing gratitude. It reminds Elizabeth, each time she receives a package, that the Lord desires gratitude from her, not because He needs to receive it, but because she will grow in His character by giving it, and will become a funnel of God's grace to others.

She lets the full impact of this flood her being as she says aloud, " He does not ask me to pay Him for my salvation, for His guidance in my walking with Him, or for the abundance of love and grace He bestows on me. He doesn't even ask me to try, since it would be impossible. Yet, it is possible to live Godly in Christ Jesus as I live by His faith and in His hope, and show His love."

Suzette is an example of a lesson in gratitude that Elizabeth expects will exhibit itself, in her, for the remainder of her life. She doesn't expect that Suzette will ever lose touch with Mama, while she does think Suzette will always encourage young girls who are fragile and appear as though they could easily go astray. She has already accepted a position in Atlanta with a large church that ministers to "up and outers," people whose lives are lush with the world's goods, but who are mostly dry deserts spiritually, often leaving their privileged children to find their own sense of direction in a world that provides too many wrong choices. Suzette keeps a close walk with the Lord and depends on two accountability partners on campus. She asks Elizabeth to pray about new ones for her in Atlanta, people whom she believes the Lord will have prepared and waiting for her upon arrival in July.

# Chapter 28

Spring break finds Elizabeth exhausted, because she has spread herself so thin. But she knows that in the long run she will thank herself a million times over for the deepening of her relationships. Mama implores her to rest for a couple of days before jumping into the jobs she invariably finds to do in Erwin. She agrees and opts to go to sleep early on her first night home, to the sights and sounds of her favorite video, "Anne of Green Gables." Mama leaves her on the couch, where she wakes early to see Mama in the kitchen preparing homemade cinnamon rolls.

"Oh, how she spoils me," Elizabeth whispers to herself as she strolls toward Mama for a hug.

"Mama," she asks, "how do you feel about us getting out those letters and cards sent to Daddy before his death? I have thought of them several times during these years back in Erwin, but it has not seemed the right time for one reason or another. I think it is time now, however."

Mama thinks it is an ideal time. So, after breakfast, they make their way up the attic ladder with Mama leading the way. She knows exactly where that box is, and instructs Elizabeth to go back down the ladder a few steps, so she can hand it down to her.

She quickly adds, "Don't open it until I get down." There is an urgency and determination in that request, or rather that command, about which Elizabeth wonders. But she doesn't question as Mama rarely does anything without an excellent reason. She waits at the bottom of the ladder for Mama to descend, so she can catch her if she falls, though she is certain that Mama goes up and down this ladder without Elizabeth more times than she would want to know.

Elizabeth carries the box, which is reminiscent of another box she and Mama once shared, to the kitchen table.

As Mama fixes them each a cup of tea from the pot of water she already has heating on the stove, Elizabeth wonders if she ever fails to think ahead.

Mama opens the box, while Elizabeth stands over her with growing anticipation, since this time has finally arrived. As Mama lifts out a bulging manila envelope and places it on the table, Elizabeth knows not to it touch yet. Then Mama takes out other envelopes, which she pronounces "off limits," and carries them to her room. Upon returning, she hands the pregnant-looking envelope to Elizabeth. As she opens the clasp, the contents begin to spill out. She looks on in amazement as Mama begins to sort them into an unlikely order.

"Mama," she says, "The envelopes have dated postmarks on them. Isn't that a logical order for reading them?"

Mama replies, "The chronology doesn't seem so important to me. There is a progression in the way you should read them, because of the way in which I think they will speak to you."

The first one Elizabeth reads is one she remembers reading

soon after father came home from the hospital, the one detailing how the Lord used her father to save a home and family. Her questioning mind wants to know where this family is now. So she asks Mama, who tells her that they are all still in Erwin, adding "You could very well run across all the boys in the course of a day."

Elizabeth takes note of the name at the bottom of the page and realizes that a young man with the same last name cuts Mama's grass every summer.

The next letter is short and quite direct. It expresses thanks for the Thanksgiving meal that her father's service station gives away every year to the person with the oldest car in Erwin. Mama sees that Elizabeth is puzzled by this one, and explains that it was a clever way to give to someone with a need by making him feel a little like a celebrity.

After that, Elizabeth reads that her father had helped the preacher enclose his carport to make a room for two unexpected nephews who came to live with them at the request of their single mother, who could not handle them alone in the midst of encroaching city influences. Her father not only helped to get a home ready for them, but he also gave the boys jobs at the station that first summer. They could not get away from Godly influences at home with the preacher and at work with Mr. Sam. In addition, before the school year began, they had both made professions of faith in Jesus.

Again, Elizabeth looks to Mama for amplification and she explains that they are now husbands and fathers. One is in seminary in Memphis, and the other manages a service station in Weaver, less than an hour away. Mama smiles as she shares that he employs a different teenage boy each summer.

One letter simply says, "Sam, I will miss you because you are my dearest friend and because you keep me answerable." It is signed " Bob."

Elizabeth realized she had never before thought of her father and his mechanics as friends, only as co-workers. Why had it not occurred to her?

Next, Mama gives her the note from Glenn, her father's other mechanic. This time, she knows what to expect, or does she? A poem is not what she expects!

"Sam, your life is a light,
Your time belongs to all.
You fight the good fight,
Determined not to fall.
Your vision is to care,
You teach me every day.
As you implore me to share
God's soul-winning way."

Though Elizabeth has often heard Glenn openly share the gospel as he waits on a customer, she has never heard him wax poetic. She gains an expanded view of him and his talents.

As much as she would like to gorge herself emotionally on these letters, as she sometimes does physically on Thanksgiving turkey, she wants to take this slowly, to absorb as much as she can and internalize as much as she needs to. Mama understands. They both realize that tears are cleansing, but they can also be draining. Elizabeth almost wishes it were time to peel and put up peaches, to help bring her emotions into check. Those peach-peeling days provide connection in a different way, through the ordinary and simple things of life.

Elizabeth has begun reading a book for pleasure, something which has not happened often lately, when Aunt Jan comes over for an update on Elizabeth and Phillip from a woman's perspective. Elizabeth laughs and recounts details that she knows Aunt Jan is itching to hear. Aunt Jan responds with a knowing smile, and presents Elizabeth with a pair of pillowcases she has embroidered. They embrace, and Mama quickly joins in to make it a group hug.

Elizabeth decides that each weekday, she will sit with Mama and they will read one more letter together, while Mama continues to fill in the gaps for her. Today, Mama's choice is another one that Elizabeth read as a child. She remembers little snatches of it as she reads about her father sharing garden land for a family whose hungry mouths doubled overnight from four to eight, when they took in family members during a crisis. Contrasted with so much emphasis on foster care today, Elizabeth begins to see how unselfishly families once took care of their own, with little concern for the hardship it brought to them. This letter, in combination with the preacher's, cuts to the core of her having fallen prey to the government's role being much more skewed than she had realized, and to the way Christians have too often relinquished their duties in caring for those in need. She is glad to have set a one-a-day limit on the letters, because each one provides for her an old remembrance or a new perspective of her father that she wants to internalize.

Throughout the break, they read four more letters covering new tires for a young woman going into the city every day for work and to take night classes, a wrecker service to Chattanooga for a young mother and her two small children who had car trouble while in Erwin visiting her ill brother, a contribution to the church for a communion table, and, Elizabeth's personal favorite, a note from Uncle Joe explaining that he respects her father for having deep convictions that cause him to do right.

As if coming home to Mama's were not enough to thrill Elizabeth, she now anticipates knowing her father better on each trip.

# Chapter 29

Back on campus, Elizabeth is ambivalent about her last few weeks. What is more important, an "A" in class or an "A" out of class? Can she do both? Perhaps she can, since Phillip is not taking up her time. His class overloads and work schedule preclude his meeting her in Erwin except on Sundays, and they truly make the most of Sundays, actually hoarding them and their time together. Being apart is proving to be progressively harder on both of them, causing Elizabeth to ask Phillip if he really needs that extra degree. He assures her that they will both be glad if he finishes, because of the advantages the degree will afford. Besides, they agree that it is right to finish what they start. Elizabeth recognizes that she is spent and will gain a better perspective after graduation. But when will Phillip have a much-needed break? Why does she wonder, as they both live by the fact that God knows all and is available to guide them, through His word, toward His best?

Phillip's semester ends a week before hers. Since his week's break coincides with her exams, he stays in Atlanta, swapping out some work hours with a friend so he can be off for her graduation weekend.

Jeannie and Elizabeth expect to see each other regularly through Jeannie's remaining college years, since she will spend much time in Erwin at Grandma's house. They will miss the daily laughing times, but mail and phone calls will help.

During the summer break, Morgan is going back to Australia, and has asked Jeannie, along with her family, to come for a visit in July, which is their dead of winter. Jeannie is ecstatic. Dr. Greene remembers his R&R there during the Vietnam War, and he expects this trip to give him more than that tourist's view through the eyes of a timid soldier. He wants to explore the backcountry, for the enjoyment of it, and to observe their medical practices.

Everyone's plans are well directed. Suzette has invited Elizabeth to stay with her in Atlanta any time she wants to visit Phillip. And, Elizabeth accepts that open invitation readily.

Sue is engaged and planning a wedding for next spring. However, her life will remain the same, in many ways, since she plans to stay and work at the college after the wedding.

Stacey is happy to be girlish again after taking on a woman's job for three years, when she was not yet a woman. She was dutiful and would not have chosen another path. Perhaps that is what makes the flexibility and carefree nature of campus life so exciting for her. She is, nevertheless, ready for the summer vacation during which she will work in her aunt's tearoom. It is a genteel place, with a British influence, which fits a bit with her love of England and her major in British literature.

Sue's apartment is the logical spot for the friends to congregate on what is their last night on campus, temporarily for some and forever for others. They are in their pajamas, and all share the remains of their stash of chocolate. As they reminisce, they laugh and cry, or laugh till they cry. The memories are bittersweet, especially for those who are graduating. The heightened excitement is slightly tempered by the nagging questions of "Are we ready?" and "We are prepared, aren't we?"

They commit to staying in touch with each other and with the Lord. That thought is the capstone of the evening, or rather the early morning. As for Elizabeth, she cannot keep her heavy lids from closing over her eyes, and she sleeps in the oversized recliner until the morning sun shining on her face wakes her. One squinty glance at her watch tells her it is 6:00.

Graduation is at 10:00, and Phillip, who went to Erwin last night, will be arriving with Mama, Aunt Jan, and Grandma around 9:00. There is no time to waste for Elizabeth. Though she packed most of her things into her car last night, there are still the last-minute things. She fixes her hair, even though it will be covered by that fashion statement, the mortarboard. Minimal make up will do for her outdoor graduation on this muggy day. She dons her gown and goes downstairs to wait for her favorite people to arrive, only to find them waiting in the lobby. Her tired eyes brighten. All her ladies give warm hugs, as Phillip waits his turn. He has no shame as he kisses her long and tenderly for all to see. The girls descending the stairs have the best view. Their applause begins a chain reaction, and Elizabeth can only smile.

The graduation ceremony is especially meaningful to her, as it represents a major milestone on the road of her hopes and dreams. She accepts her diploma proudly, smiling at Mama, and winking at Phillip as she leaves the stage. They all stop by the reception briefly, to allow Elizabeth to thank as many faculty and staff members as is feasible, for enriching her college days.

In some ways, college ended too soon for Elizabeth. She has needed the safe grandmothering she received from Mama, and she is not certain she is ready to relinquish even a small bit of it for full-fledged adulthood.

# Chapter 30

Once home, Phillip takes all the cars to be gassed up and cleaned. While he is gone, Elizabeth sneaks in a little nap, and being more tired than she realized, she sleeps right through Phillip's visit with Mama when he returns. During this time he tells her that he doesn't know quite how to go about asking for Elizabeth's hand in marriage. He explains to Mama that though he is very comfortable with her, and though he fully expects she is pleased with him as the future husband of Elizabeth, he thinks this situation doesn't fit protocol.

Mama agrees. She stands, and announces that she will be right back. Returning from her room, she carries a manila envelope addressed to "Elizabeth's Suitor." Phillip scrutinizes it at length after Mama places it in his hand.

As he looks up at Mama, she answers his question before he asks. "Phillip, Elizabeth's father wrote this letter for you when Elizabeth was eight years old. I have never read it, though it has been in my possession for fifteen years and is not sealed. It is not written to me; it was only entrusted to me to present to the right person at the right time. You may want to read it out on the swing or under the big tree at Jan's. Well, what I am trying to say is that I think it is private."

Phillip nods and rushes over to the glider under the big tree. He wants to tear into the envelope and devour the letter, but apprehension overtakes him. Could he be any more nervous if he were speaking to Elizabeth's father in person? He prays for the Lord to calm him and prepare him for this mysterious and unusual letter. Finally, his hands untuck the fold, being careful not to wrinkle the envelope as he slowly slides out the one-page letter obviously written by a shaky hand, but composed by the clear head of a loving father.

"Dear Man of My Girl's Heart,

"I long to know you, but that will only happen in eternity. I trust that my Elizabeth will choose, for a husband, a man who loves the Lord intensely and walks with Him daily. I expect she will choose a man who exhibits his love for her in the way that he leads, protects, and cherishes her. I think she will choose a man of honor who is easy to respect and love.

"Since my Elizabeth chooses you, I cannot imagine that you will not fit the above description, but in the unlikely event that you do not, please tell her that you made a mistake, and exit from her life. If you do fit the above description, as I strongly expect that you do, you have my complete blessing. You also have my respect as you take the position of leadership that was mine for such a short time, the position that I would be handing over to you at the wedding, if I were there.

"As I write this letter, I give to you, now, my abundant love.
The Former Man of Your Girl's Heart"

Phillip grasps the full impact instantly. He sees that there is caution coupled with an overriding trust. He will use it as accountability in his marriage, from the wedding day till the Lord takes him home. He bounds up the steps to Aunt Jan's porch two at a time, asking her to fix cold lemonade while he calls Mama to come over. He can hardly contain his excitement, as he paces the floor for those few dragging minutes it takes the three of them to settle down at the kitchen table.

Phillip reads the letter aloud and proclaims that, although he has not had a conventional father-son relationship with his own dedicated father and has only vague boyhood memories of Elizabeth's father, they have both given him the example of, and the charge to, unwavering love and stability. He says they have been, and will continue to be, fathers to emulate, by their responses to the life God allowed for them.

Phillip excuses himself to put the letter in a safe drawer of Aunt Jan's file cabinet, and goes to his bedroom to contemplate ways to share the letter with Elizabeth.

At Mama's, Elizabeth is startled awake by a racing motorcycle. As she stretches and gazes out the open blinds, she sees Mama making her way home from the visit at Aunt Jan's. Mama stops and sits a while in the porch swing, reflecting on the letter Phillip has just shared.

Suddenly, Elizabeth and her pillow are joining Mama in the swing, pushing it far higher than Mama's comfort level allows on this particular day. Mama moves to the rocker, and they talk. Elizabeth's words run over each other, which is her way when she is excited.

She catches Mama up on the latest of every girl who has ever visited in her home. Mama wants more, and she pumps Elizabeth for details and feelings. Mama already knows more about Suzette than Elizabeth does, as they will be bonded until Mama's dying day. She probably is as informed about Jeannie as Elizabeth is, because of Grandma. Finally, Elizabeth realizes it is not information that Mama is looking for, it is intimacy. She wants it for Elizabeth more than for herself, as she continues to build trust in Elizabeth that will spill over into future relationships. It takes time to build unshakeable trust, but Mama is a builder. Although even she will be surprised at how soon her building skills will be tested.

# Chapter 31

Phillip has toyed with several ideas concerning how to present the ring to Elizabeth, but none has seemed exactly right. Since receiving and digesting her father's letter, he wonders if he should include it also. He rules out a fancy restaurant as impersonal, with strangers only a few feet away. He wonders if a picnic on the lake is special enough, since they do that so often, or does the fact that they do it often make it the perfect setting? He could simply fall to his knees in front of her in Mama's living room and propose the old-fashioned way, since Elizabeth is an old-fashioned girl. How could he not yet have the perfect plan, when he has worked on it diligently? Phillip revisits a plan of suspense and levity that he concocted early on, but had abandoned as too risky. He reasons that they both have been so inundated with seriousness that they are losing their sense of humor, so maybe this plan is the way to go.

He also reasons that since time is of the essence, and since two Christians becoming engaged could be considered a spiritual experience, he will not fret over making dinner cruise reservations that conflict with evening church next Sunday.

That evening, they all overeat Aunt Jan's meal of country

fried steak and gravy with the creamiest mashed potatoes and some of her home-canned green beans, and topped off with peach cobbler. Then Elizabeth and Phillip stroll the neighborhood, stopping by Mrs. Carter's for a short visit. She has a graduation gift for Elizabeth, a framed cross-stitch of one of her favorite verses, Colossians 3:4, "When Christ who is our life, shall appear, then shall ye also appear with him in glory." Elizabeth is abundant in her gratitude and in her affection, as always, for Mrs. Carter.

Returning to Mama's, they sit on the swing, the place Elizabeth deems the most relaxing in all of Erwin, perhaps, in all of the world. The soothing sound of silence surrounds them. It is the perfect setting for two young people in love, but still it does not make their time together linger long enough.

Sunday morning church brings not only a message of hope, but also a stream of congratulations and gifts for Elizabeth's graduation. She feels loved, but no more by the attention and gifts of today than any other Sunday.

Phillip and Elizabeth leave at 4:00 so that they will arrive at the riverboat by 5:00.

As the hostess escorts them to their table, they find themselves to be magnificently situated between the stage and a view of the water, an amazing spot considering theirs was a last-minute reservation. Phillip did, however, explain the occasion and ask for a specific floral arrangement at their table.

Whatever the reason, Elizabeth views what she believes to be her graduation dinner as perfect, so far. Phillip reaches around the two red roses joined together by red organdy ribbon to take both Elizabeth's hands in his, proclaiming that the roses represent the two of them as they stand together in closeness and beauty. She is impressed with his poetry. The showboat musical captures their attention with its lively tunes from Gershwin, the food is fancy, and the service is impeccable.

After the program, they wander out on the deck and Phillip removes the clip from Elizabeth's hair to let it blow in the breeze like her wispy, pale pink sundress, making her a picture of romance. Eventually, they position themselves beside the rail, mesmerized by the gentle movement of the water, as it sparkles in the moonlight. Phillip takes the ring case from his pants pocket, and slowly opens the velvet box displaying the ring, which also sparkles in the moonlight. Elizabeth's eyes, too, are sparkling in the moonlight.

Just as Phillip removes the ring from the box, he fumbles and drops it overboard. Elizabeth shrieks with shock, then cries at the loss and emotional pain for both of them.

Phillip looks at her in the midst of her frantic tears and asks, "Will you marry me anyway …… without a ring?"

She is puzzled and annoyed by the fact that he, seemingly, has no regrets over losing this obviously expensive ring, which he worked so hard to afford. Now, Phillip is afraid to tell Elizabeth the truth, that the ring floating to the bottom of the lake is a fake and the real one is in another pocket.

Phillip asks himself what he could have been thinking as Elizabeth drops into a nearby chair, still crying softly.

"Lord," he pleads silently, "Please take my mess and show me how to turn it into the sweetness that Elizabeth desires and deserves." Next, Phillip takes the real ring out of his pocket and holds it out of sight until he thinks the time is right.

Cautiously, he humbles himself by kneeling before Elizabeth and taking her left hand with his free hand. He looks deep into her hurting eyes and wants to brush her still flowing tears away. He doesn't attempt to open this box, but simply places it into her lap where her gaze is focused. She stares at it for what seems like half of eternity.

Her hand caresses the small box, and it becomes apparent to Phillip that she thinks this is the original box that did not go overboard with the ring. The joke now seems more cruel than before.

Phillip silently petitions the Lord again, saying, "Lord, I am still trying to pull something romantic out of this, but it doesn't seem to be working. Help me to think of a way to rectify this."

By the time he has articulated the prayer in his mind, he sees Elizabeth's quiet disappointment and confusion turn to action. She clutches the box in her hand and says, "You might as well throw the box away, too."

She lifts the box to toss it just as Phillip catches her arm. The box drops to the deck and falls open. This ring, too, glistens in the moonlight and catches Elizabeth's eye. They reach for it simultaneously, but Phillip is closer. He picks up the ring, and tells her that he thinks he wants to save it for another time. She agrees. They embrace, ending their first serious argument, and hoping there is never another one so intense.

On the way home, Phillip tells Elizabeth the entire story of how he thought they needed some lightness in their lives, and thought adding frivolity to the proposal was the answer.

"When it got out of hand," Phillip says, "I prayed twice for the Lord to rescue me and restore the situation. At first, I wondered why He did not seem to help, but now I am convinced that He wants me to understand that sometimes there are natural consequences for our folly. Practical jokes have their place, but this was not the place. Becoming officially engaged should be a moment a woman can remember fondly, and share tenderly with her daughters and granddaughters. I think someday that we will laugh uproariously about tonight and its comedy of errors. But, I think a new and proper proposal is in order."

She nods in agreement.

"Next time, Elizabeth, you will have a night to remember fondly," Phillip assures her.

# Chapter 32

Bright and early on Monday morning, as Phillip climbs into the driver's seat and starts the engine for the lonely ride back to Emory for his first class at 1:00, Elizabeth wants to jump in the passenger seat and never be separated from him again.

At breakfast, she tells Mama the gory and glory details of last night. Mama reaches for her hand across the table and squeezes it knowingly, understanding that Elizabeth and Phillip's love was not threatened by the fiasco, but realizing that Elizabeth's trust was compromised by having this momentous event treated without its due respect. They sit in silence as Mama gathers her thoughts.

"Elizabeth," Mama begins, "You have told me that you did kiss and make up, that Phillip realizes the hurt caused by a joke at such a tender time, and that he plans to propose in a most appropriate way in the near future; but I sense more than your romantic dream was lost. I believe that a bit of trust was also lost. Elizabeth, we both know that humans are perfect only in position and not in condition. We are going to fail. We are especially going to fail the ones with whom we share the deepest love and the most intricate intimacies of mind and heart. When that hurt comes to us, it creates turbulence in us like a boat in a storm.

"This is a time to remember who steadies our boat. Picture Jesus and his disciples on the stormy sea. The disciples were frantic, but not Jesus. He knew that He could ride them through the storm, or He could calm the storm. Either way, it was about those disciples learning to trust Him. Today, our walk is still about building trust in Him. When we walk by faith, we are lining up our lives with the privileged position we have in our living Lord. Although Phillip is not the Lord, the need to build trust in him also is a necessary component for walking well together into your future."

Mama pauses, then adds, "Don't let negative thoughts roll around in your head, gathering momentum and adding embellishments, until they eventually distort the truth and leave little room for the fresh and positive aspects of each new day."

Mama leaves Elizabeth to her thoughts on their conversation, while she slips into her outdoor shoes and heads for the garden to pull the grass and weeds from her new spring plants. It is a satisfying job for her, a place where she thinks and prays uninterrupted. Today, though, she has to laugh at the cleverness of Phillip's ill-fated humor. She knows Phillip and Elizabeth will be fine, because he is already broken up over hurting his beloved, and she is presently sorting through the emotion, to the solid foundation of Christ that has carried her through the loss of both parents, years of an insecure lifestyle, and nagging questions of rejection. That foundation also will carry her through whatever is next.

When Mama comes in for a cool drink and a little rest, Elizabeth is putting on her gardening clothes. Mama says that she is done for today, and wonders if Elizabeth wants to drive her on errands. The answer to that question is a resounding, "Yes!" because Elizabeth loves to drive Mama's stick shift.

She also knows that Monday's errands involve driving to Uncle Jimmy's to pick up fresh goat's milk for her neighbor, whose little boy is allergic to cow's milk. The neighbor could go herself, but Mama likes the consistency of seeing her brother every week. They delight in reminiscing, which is a combination history and genealogy lesson for Elizabeth.

Today, for instance, they decide to take a drive to the cemetery to place flowers on the graves of Papa and Aunt Mary Mae. Part of Elizabeth wonders why people visit cemeteries, since the corpses don't even know they are there. Mama's answer is that the visit is not for the dead, but for the living. Tombstones can tell a person a lot, but if a family historian comes along and relates stories about each person, a richness is added to the life of the listener.

Uncle Jimmy is the best at remembering and recounting old stories. Often, he tells the same ones over and over, causing them to have a life of their own. Things jog his memory, depending on the time of year, whose birthday it is, the weather, the mood he is in, or some other variable, and he relates a totally new story. This time, though, Mama tells the story.

Standing by Papa's grave, she asks Uncle Jimmy, "Do you remember the time you and Johnny were killing hogs at Grandpa's house? Johnny blew up the hog bladder, tied a knot in it like a balloon, and threw it at you. But, Mrs. O'Dell, dressed in her finery as a Watkins saleslady, had just stepped out of the house to return to her car, and she took the hit. It knocked her off balance and one of her high-heeled shoes got caught on an exposed root. She fell to the ground and her pocketbook flew into the air, spilling all of its contents. She righted herself, brushed off her clothes, and refused your help in gathering her belongings.

"We ladies saw it all from the window, but knew it was a scene that we were not even to speak of, much less be a part of. I think today is the first time that story has crossed my lips, but I figure it is safe to tell it now, since Mrs. O'Dell has spent the last twenty years right here in this cemetery with her attacker."

Mama chuckles, and Elizabeth does not know whether it is at the silliness of the scene so long ago, or if it is at her own clever quip about where Mrs. O'Dell has spent the last twenty years.

After delivering the milk and stopping by the grocery store for a few items, they arrive home to find company on the porch. Jeannie is swinging and Grandma is rocking. Elizabeth carries the groceries in, and pours lemonade for four. When she returns, she sees Aunt Jan making her way over. She leaves her glass for Aunt Jan and starts back to pour another, when she notices Jeannie following her. She clearly wants to talk privately, so they make a detour to Elizabeth's bedroom.

Jeannie is so proficient with her prosthesis now, that she can practically leave Elizabeth in the dust as they navigate the narrow hallway. Jeannie wants to talk about Morgan, relating for Elizabeth once more how they had decided that theirs was only a friendship. Jeannie was fine with that, since she fully expected it to develop into more at the ideal time. Yet, Morgan told her just before she left campus that he has a girlfriend at home, and he wanted her to know that before she and her family arrive in July.

Confusion now reigns in Jeannie's mind over this. He has

never mentioned a girlfriend before. Why would he invite her and her family for a visit if he were in a relationship? Is she simply a crippled young girl for whom he feels sorry? Why did this conversation not come up until the eleventh hour? She feels betrayed, though she has no grounds for feeling betrayed. Morgan was never dishonest with her. It was her own expectations that betrayed her.

"Elizabeth," she asks, "is being grown up always going to be this emotional? I thought the teen years were supposed to be the emotional ones. I am twenty-one. What is this confusion and uncertainty about? I have been able to bounce back from anything, and I have never had a problem with trust before."

Elizabeth is more than grateful for Mama's pep talk this morning. Now she can pass it on to Jeannie. Or perhaps Jeannie would prefer to hear those words from Mama herself. But Jeannie asks her to keep it just between the two of them for now, then listens as Elizabeth repeats, as closely as she can, Mama's lesson on trust.

"The question is," Elizabeth asks, "do you still plan to go to Australia knowing what you know? Morgan obviously thinks nothing of it, as he continued to talk about your trip after breaking the news of his girlfriend. Of course, you have not discussed it with your parents, have you? Jeannie, this whole turn of events needs time. Time is a stabilizer. Time is our friend."

Jeannie breathes a sigh of relief and commits to waiting patiently. They hug each other, these two best girlfriends.

At supper, Elizabeth asks Mama if she wants to get out their next letter. They all touch Elizabeth's heart, but the best one this week is from Grandma, who thanks Sam for doing things for her that her own child would do if she were here, but she is not.

Elizabeth likes reading only one letter a day, even though she is eager to know more. Little does she know what future letters have in store for her.

# Chapter 33

As Phillip arrives on Sunday morning just in time for Sunday School, he finds Elizabeth in her classroom of fourth, fifth, and sixth-graders. They beam, because they like him and they enjoy his storytelling, which makes the Scriptures come alive for them. Immediately, they beg him to tell them about the Red Sea parting, and Elizabeth gladly defers to them and him. Watching him fascinates Elizabeth, and she is once again drawn to his careful detail in relating the stories of the Bible. Mama said that she must watch for opportunities to rebuild trust, and this is one. She sees how she can trust him with the excitement and truth of God's word in the lives of young children.

The summer moves rapidly by, and Phillip has yet to mention the ring again. Little does Elizabeth know that he is checking with Mama about the wisest time to bring it up, and she gives him a weekly barometer reading. She tells him he is on his own as to how he will present it this time, but she is confident he will find the ideal way.

Summer progresses as usual, with Mama and Elizabeth peeling and putting up peaches, and Elizabeth continuing to clean for "her ladies."

Elizabeth calculates that by continuing to read one letter a day with Mama, they will last until fall arrives, which is a perfect way to round out their summer together. One day, Elizabeth asks Mama if she thinks it will be okay to share them with Phillip the next time she reads through them, and Mama determines that her father would like that.

It is a sultry evening as Mama, Elizabeth, and Aunt Jan, who could cool themselves in the air-conditioned house, choose instead to enjoy the breeze from the oscillating fan blowing over them on the porch as they swing and sip lemonade. The phone rings, and Elizabeth rushes to answer, finding Jeannie on the other line.

She and her family are just back from Australia. It was her choice not to tell her parents about Morgan's girlfriend, and to go as the dutiful friend so as not to disappoint her father, who had become so fond Morgan, and who had his heart set on the medical "field trip" into the bush.

From the initial sound of Jeannie's voice, Elizabeth is sure that the girlfriend episode turned out to be a non-issue. Jeannie jumps into that, first thing. Upon arrival, Jeannie tells her that she follows her self-prescribed course of extreme frivolity. Morgan's parents are quickly drawn to her good humor, joining in her fun and pulling her into theirs. On their fourth day in this fascinating country, Morgan's brother and sister-in-law, with their seven boys ages two through fourteen and a baby girl, still new enough to be pink and soft, arrive early to spend the entire day. Morgan laughs and rough-houses with the nephews, giving full attention to each. Next, he shakes hands with his brother, Matt, and kisses Debbie on the forehead. Then, with great aplomb, he lifts little Megan into the air before settling her cheek next to his and announcing as he looks straight into Jeannie's eyes, "Meet my girlfriend!"

Laughter fills the room, but the happiness filling Jeannie's heart truly betrays her insistence that Morgan is only her friend. She renews her expectation for romance.

Morgan explains to them that Megan is the first girl born into their family since the birth of his great-grandmother, who is ninety-four. As he talks, Mrs. Price brings out a picture of the five generations, with their Nana and Megan being the center of attention among the three men.

Jeannie cannot say that anything dynamic happened between her and Morgan during the visit, but Morgan did tell her that he would be ready for another fun-filled year together. The remainder of her conversation with Elizabeth is idle chitchat with a promise to give her friend the details, when she brings Grandma back to Erwin next week.

# Chapter 34

Phillip has three days between the summer and fall sessions. He naturally wants to spend it in Erwin, but he is drawn to go home for a visit with his father and mother, whom he feels he has neglected lately, just as he feels about Elizabeth in the midst of his over-scheduled schedule. He asks Elizabeth if she will meet him there, since her introduction to his family is overdue.

Phillip adds, "And, there is that incidental benefit for the two of us to spend time together."

Elizabeth arrives in Charleston several hours before Phillip and makes her way to the nursing home where Phillip's mother has spent most of her adulthood, finding that it is clean and pleasant and happy. Elizabeth wonders if it is all right for her to visit Mrs. Winn without any family members there, since she doesn't know her. She decides to take the chance. Upon entering the room, Elizabeth sees pictures of Phillip everywhere and quickly recognizes the ones taken of him when he was a toddler.

Elizabeth positions herself in front of Mrs. Winn's wheelchair and smiles, receiving a smile in return. When she reaches for Mrs. Winn's hand, she finds it icy cold, and warms it up between her own hands as she introduces herself and recounts several incidents in her relationship with Phillip.

Mrs. Winn clangs her right foot on the wheelchair and makes low gurgling noises at the sound of her son's name. This tells Elizabeth that someone is keeping precious moments alive in her twisted body and imprisoned brain. She finds herself drawn to Phillip's mother in an indescribable way, and is just leaning over to kiss her hand when Phillip and his father enter.

His father looks surprised, and wonders if this warmly attentive young woman is a new therapist. Phillip introduces Elizabeth, and his father's expression assures her that she is indeed welcome into this room and into this family.

In the evening, Phillip and his father take Elizabeth to meet the aunts, uncles, and cousins living nearby. They ride from house to house, dropping in unannounced, but unquestionably welcome. Phillip's family is undaunted by spontaneity and eagerly accepting of a stranger. No wonder Phillip has often talked about how much family support he had growing up, with his mother extremely ill and his father dedicated to her care.

The next day when they visit his mother, the staff has dressed her, at Phillip's request, in a pale blue outfit with small, feminine ruffles, to fit his view of her softness. Elizabeth is animated with her, which elicits a big smile. It is obvious that they like each other, as they sit side by side in front of the window with a blooming rose garden as their backdrop. When Phillip's father arrives, he is also dressed up at Phillip's request. Actually, Elizabeth is also dressed up, at Phillip's request. She looks around and sees that Phillip has brought his camera, so she asks what the special occasion is.

At that very moment, Phillip hands the camera to a strategically placed staff member and bends on one knee in front of his Mother and Elizabeth. He strokes his mother's face and then takes Elizabeth's left hand in his, placing the engagement ring on her finger while asking, "Elizabeth, will you marry me?"

An affirmative nod is all she can manage in the throes of emotion surrounding this entire scene.

Phillip stands, lifts Elizabeth to her feet, and into his embrace, for a kiss that beats the one in the woods she had previously pronounced as unbeatable. Much of the staff is now standing in the doorway clapping, and Phillip's mother is clanging her leg brace on her wheelchair while his father simply smiles.

Back at home, Phillip asks his father to join them. Then he sits between his father and Elizabeth and lays the manila envelope on the kitchen table. He explains how Mama gave it to him; and carefully, to show respect, he takes the letter out and reads it aloud to them.

Phillip tells Elizabeth that his father's undying love for his mother, and her father's foresight in leaving this epistle of Godly instruction, is more than most men get in a lifetime, yet he has it to begin his role as her husband. He commits to Elizabeth to honor her father's requests and aims to lead her well in the Lord. He reaches for her hand and his father's and prays a prayer of gratitude.

Phillip leaves late the next night while Elizabeth stays two more days with his cousin, Lyn, who is already married and the mother of two small children, though she is the same age as Elizabeth. The two become fast friends as Lyn draws Elizabeth into her life.

Lyn seems to have a knack for doing it all. She keeps a clean and orderly house, has mannerly and obedient children, and fixes great meals. Elizabeth asks her how she does it, and she explains that she keeps her life uncluttered from excess and focuses on what is most important. Sometimes she feels an urgency, but rarely. She thinks she learned it from Phillip's father, whose focus never wavered. She was continually impressed at the way he maintained his calm when the movers and shakers were often in a state of panic. "Life can often be simple if we do not make it complicated," Lyn tells Elizabeth.

Elizabeth is impressed and wants to learn from her. She gets Lyn's phone number so they can talk. Not only is Elizabeth an engaged woman now, but she is already feeling included in her new family-to-be.

Elizabeth returns to the nursing home one more time, before leaving town for the long drive home. She is once more animated, and again finds Phillip's mother is responsive to her. Elizabeth aches for all Mrs. Winn has missed, due to the illness that has encased her, but she sees how the Lord has used it for everyone whose life she touches. She even sees a joy present in Mrs. Winn that she has seen in very few healthy women. No one knows what is in store for a particular life, nor does one understand all of life's whys, but this truth is knowable: God is the great I AM and that interprets all else. This life is not all there is, not nearly all there is. After a lengthy visit, Elizabeth kisses her future mother-in-law goodbye, and forces herself to leave.

The drive back seems shorter than its actual miles, as Elizabeth has much to think about and sort through. She was almost ready to talk to Mama concerning getting a job in the fall, but now she wonders if her volunteer work, visiting Phillip's family more, and planning the wedding will keep her busy enough. Even considering all of these things, however, does not touch the real reason for not wanting a job. The real reason is she wants to spend as much time with Mama as she can from now until the wedding, because she expects to be moving away, so life will no longer offer them the same camaraderie. Elizabeth is not afraid to work and does not want a reputation of slothfulness. She will do any job Mama has for her, or any jobs for Aunt Jan and her other ladies. She will clean the service station or perform some other mundane job that Bob and Glenn have for her. She simply wants time to soak up the warmth in this gentle town a while longer.

# Chapter 35

Mama is more than a little glad to see Elizabeth turn in the driveway. She has covered a lot of miles today, and the highways are crowded. Mama meets her on the steps and takes one of her bags, immediately putting it down on the porch to hug and kiss her.

Mama does not know about the ring, as Phillip saved the news for Elizabeth to tell, knowing she would want to share the news with Mama, herself. However, Mama knew that it could happen anytime, since she had told Phillip a couple of weeks ago that she thought Elizabeth had regained her trust in him, due to both their efforts.

As Mama bends to pick the bag up again, she sees the ring, but says nothing, even though her mind is screaming to be heard. She rushes to put the bag into Elizabeth's room, in order to expedite the announcement. As she turns toward the door, she finds Elizabeth's hand in her face. Elizabeth guides Mama two steps backward and gives her a tiny shove onto the bed, then jumps over her to the other side and plumps up their pillows.

"Remember, Mama, how we used to lie in bed when I was little and talk about important things?"

Mama laughs, and settles herself comfortably into Elizabeth's plan. Elizabeth turns on the bedside lamp, positioning her hand to take advantage of the bright lighting. The princess-cut stone glistens atop its high-pronged gold mounting. This ring, so at home on Elizabeth's long finger, was truly worth the wait.

As she delights in describing the proposal, leaving no detail wanting, she continues to flash her ring under the light. She describes every person she met for Mama, expounding on the unique traits of each. Recounting her conversations shows that she has rehearsed them repeatedly in her mind to retain all facts and feelings. She aptly compares the different homes to ones in Erwin, providing a clear mental picture for Mama, except that she cannot express, to her satisfaction, the thrill of meeting Phillip's mother. There are no words in her vocabulary to articulate the intricacies of communication that passed between the two of them. Yes, laughter is the universal language, even for those who have no voice. But, there was more, a mysterious and hidden language that seemed to belong to the two of them alone. Mama feels as if she has been there. She wishes she had been there, but is content to know the trip provided several pieces to fit into the puzzle of Elizabeth's life.

# Chapter 36

Phillip begins the fall semester with his heaviest class load ever. If he can manage it, he will be finished in December. College life was fun before, but real adulthood is his mindset now. He has found the woman of his dreams, and he is ready for what is next. He is prepared in his mind and heart to take a wife, but still preparing financially to care for a wife. His resolve in the Lord is strong, knowing that he and Elizabeth are facing several months of intense "busyness" in separate places. Reality deems that the stress will take its toll on them, as will having only snatches of time together, and realizing that even those times will experience legitimate infringement. But they both will remember that their goal is to get to the wedding day with their testimony intact, not marred by wrong responses to the ever-encroaching stresses.

On this first Sunday after Phillip begins his final semester, they spend a breezy, but still too hot, afternoon sitting in the swing with a man-sized calendar on their laps, searching for a wedding date.

"Phillip," Elizabeth asks, "Before we pick a date, don't we need to agree explicitly on the size of the wedding in terms of the wedding party and the guest list? It matters if we think your mother can be included in the festivities. Do we want the ceremony and reception simple or elaborate? The answer to these and other questions will determine how much time we need for planning and executing."

"Executing sounds ominous," Phillip responds with a glint in his eye.

Elizabeth laughs, and they both realize that humor will be their best friend from now until the big day. She understands that Phillip views wedding planning as the woman's domain, but sees that the basics must be agreed on by both for the details to fall into place.

Concerning Phillip's mother, the choice is made for them by calling his father, who explains that visits like the ones Elizabeth enjoyed recently are the best for her. Although the family is still learning, even after a quarter century, what works and what doesn't, they learned early on that crowds and being out of her small world are agitating to her. That means even for this momentous event, there will be no need to make accommodations for an invalid. It also means that the wedding will be in Erwin, with a much larger guest list than if they had chosen to marry in Charleston.

This plan has now been logistically simplified, but it is emotionally difficult for Elizabeth. Mama reminds her that Phillip has experienced that same feeling of living in two worlds, almost exclusive of each other, and he has found the balance. Mama reminds her that in the Lord is where we find perfect balance. Hers will not be the same as Phillip's just as Phillip's is not the same as his father's, who is to be commended and admired for his choice to make his wife's world his world.

Elizabeth and Phillip decide on two tentative dates. The first date, December 19, will mean ultra organization and heightened activity on her part for planning the wedding, as well as on his part for finding the right job and perhaps relocating. The second date, March 13, is a trade-off, reducing some stress levels and intensifying others. They pray for enough information to make wise decisions before next Sunday, which is the deadline they have set for themselves to make a final choice.

Elizabeth's mind is consumed with the wedding, but not to the exclusion of reading her father's cards. That is a delightful routine for her and Mama, and after eating breakfast and cleaning up the kitchen, they have their private devotions, then meet back for the next installment. Today's pick is elementary in its wording, spelling, and penciled handwriting on notebook paper.

"Hi Mr. Sam,

"I am so sorry you are sick cause I like you.

I like to come and get gas at your gas stashun with my brother in his pickup truk.

I am in Lizabeths room at school.

I like her differnt from the way I like you.

I like her for my girlfrend.

I think she is so nice cause you are so nice.

I hope you get well soon.

Buddy"

"Oh, I remember Buddy," shouts Elizabeth. "He was the boy in my class who always chewed on his shirt collar. Mrs. Berkey embarrassed him over it, providing laughs for the class;

but I felt sad for him. Once I put my collar in my mouth at recess and chewed it to make him feel better. Back in class, Mrs. Berkey noticed my wet, scrunched- up collar, and asked if Buddy had been chewing my collar, too. I felt the hot sting of embarrassment rise till my face burned crimson. It endeared me to Buddy from then until I moved away. Does he still live around here? What is he doing now?"

"When he is not running a collar repair service out of his home, he works for UPS in Nashville." Mama replies with a wink." He met his wife at Beulah Baptist Church in Dickson, where she is the pastor's secretary and they actively attend church."

"The most interesting item of information I have about Buddy, though, is that the letter we just read together is what inspired your father to write the letter that recently became Phillip's blessing for your coming marriage. On one of those long nights," Mama chokes, then continues, "when Sam could seemingly get no relief from the pain, he expressed to me that he thought the time for his going home was near and lamented that he would have so little influence on you and your big decisions in life. He rested in the fact that you had made that all-important eternal decision to accept Christ as your Savior. Yet he knew there were other decisions which would influence the direction of your life, and which he wanted to impact for good. As weak as he was, he wanted that letter in his own handwriting, and he wanted to finish it immediately, just in case."

Elizabeth cannot stop the quiet tears from spilling over and wetting her cheeks.

Mama slides her chair closer to Elizabeth and leans over to gain her full attention as she speaks. "You have been and will continue to be impacted by your father all your earthly days. His blood courses through your veins. You have his personality. You walk in his footsteps with every act of service. Do not misunderstand me, it is the Lord who formed you in your mother's womb, but He chose you to be innately so much like your father. Perhaps He did that simply for your pleasure, or perhaps for more eternal purposes." Mama hugs Elizabeth and exits, giving her time and space, and confirming Aunt Jan's continual marveling that Mama's timing is amazing.

The routines of the week are intact, but must be escalated to make room for looking through bridal magazines, as well as making out guest lists and a myriad of other things that can be done without a firm date. Either date requires focus and action. And both require things to run smoothly. But will they?

# Chapter 37

Aunt Jan fixes Sunday dinner for the four of them and serves the dessert on a crystal dish purported to be a wedding gift to Phillip's great-great-grandmother. As they eat the apple dumplings, Aunt Jan shares the story, explaining that she had eagerly listened to it time after time.

"Great-Gram lived in near poverty conditions on the coast of Georgia, though she spoke of a genteel heritage, lost by her husband's vices. Land was wealth, but his inherited wealth decreased in proportion to the increase in his gambling debts. The land was eventually gone, and there was nothing left to pay with except the family finery.

Once, Great-Gramp wrapped this dish in a horse blanket and carried it with him to a card game, but his debt was too high for the winner to be appeased by the sparkle of "woman's stuff." He shot Great-Gramp and walked out, leaving the crystal intact on the table."

Elizabeth's eyes grow wide, while Phillip smiles at this scene before him, so similar to others throughout his life in which Aunt Jan recounted "the saving of the dish." His smile has nothing to do with being callous toward the tragedy of the story, but with the fact that he has heard it so often, it has become a legend. Mostly though, this time, his smile comes from knowing that today the story will end differently.

Aunt Jan continues, " Great-Gramp died before the doctor arrived. His last words were, 'Tell my wife I love her.' which most thinking people believe was added to the story to bring some sensitivity to his departure.

"After the funeral, another of the gamblers brought the crystal dish home to the distraught family in the same horse blanket, which Great-Gramp had used to safely carry it away. When it was unwrapped and found to be perfect, it became a symbol of survival for the family. It has been carefully used by each succeeding generation on birthdays and holidays and other special occasions, and remains today without a chip to mar its beauty or shatter its strength of purpose."

Elizabeth asks, "Since this is not a birthday or holiday, what special occasion are we celebrating?"

Aunt Jan becomes more animated as she stands and states with long-contained excitement, "Today is the day Phillip has heard about his entire life. Today is the day this symbol of strength is passed to the next generation."

With fanfare, Aunt Jan presents the crystal dish, holding the remains of half an unclaimed apple dumpling, to Phillip. He in turn presents it to Elizabeth, proclaiming with a voice of authority and importance, "The family tradition will continue."

Her uneasy response is, "Oh, Phillip, what if I break it?"

Aunt Jan assures Elizabeth that she will be on hand in the

kitchen later to supervise her first washing of the dish. The teasing and laughter do not lighten Elizabeth's heaviness. Only when Phillip tells her that the story is phony and was begun by his great uncle for fun one Thanksgiving, does Elizabeth join in the laughter.

Phillip goes on to explain that the dish does have sentimental value, however, since it had belonged to his great-aunt, who had no children of her own and passed her treasured family pieces to Aunt Jan. "It does indeed represent strength and beauty to my ancestors, and will represent strength and beauty to us," he says.

The choosing of a wedding date looms larger this week than the last to Elizabeth, but not to Phillip. He has news that he has been saving since Tuesday to deliver in person.

Out of fourteen resumes sent over the past month, Phillip heard from two more this week. It was immediately clear that one was not right for him, as it would require him to travel, at least four days a week, in addition to occasional extended trips.

The other, however, has great possibility. The home office, where he would work, is in downtown Atlanta. Good news about the location is that his current apartment would be ideal. Additionally, he is already adept at maneuvering through the Atlanta traffic. The beginning salary is small, but carries the commitment of a substantial raise after three months.

A former classmate has been with the company and reports that the workload is heavy, but the office atmosphere is not. Phillip can look forward to beginning immediately after finishing classes in December, with the promise of a week off for the wedding and honeymoon, which will not be counted into his first-year vacation package. The company benefits are conducive to family planning.

Phillip knows that warts will show up as time goes by and projects develop, but everything he considers to be essential has checked out well. Because of his international studies and the specific focus of his master's work, the company views him as having interests and a background that are advantageous to them.

Elizabeth has inadvertently tuned out since she heard that they could live in Phillip's current apartment. That piece of information alone lends itself to the December wedding date. Her mind runs rampant, from wedding dresses to apartment decorating to telling Mama to…

Phillip's mention of her name suddenly pulls her back to the conversation at hand, "It seems like a fit to me, Elizabeth, but I want us both to pray about it before I give my answer on Thursday."

"Oh, it is not definite?" she asks with a hint of concern.

"No, Elizabeth, you know we pray about everything together."

"I have prayed about our life together, daily, many times a day," she responds. "As soon as you began, I thought, 'this is an answer to my prayers,' because nothing about it conflicts with scripture for today and much about it fits our parameters."

"Elizabeth, you are probably right, especially since we have both prayed consistently, and since I see no red flags in this offer. Still, before my appointment on Thursday, let's not make plans based on this job."

Elizabeth nods in agreement, knowing that she will not make concrete plans, while also knowing that dreams of how it might work will fill her mind from now until then.

# Chapter 38

It is a long week, as the days and nights drag by. Finally, Thursday arrives, and the phone rings before breakfast is over. It is Phillip touching base with Elizabeth to confirm that they are on the same page before he finalizes his plans for this position.

Phillip enters his meeting with confidence that he is exactly where he should be. The salary, as previously stated, is put into writing, and the benefits package is clear. A copy of the company policy is now in his possession, and he takes a preference test to guide the company with his client assignments. All is quite the same as presented in the past, except for the beginning date, which has been pushed to January 4, to avoid beginning in the midst of a major holiday.

Soon, Phillip calls to say that he has taken the position. Since he is late for class, he says he will share details with Elizabeth on Sunday, but he quickly states that plans can begin for a December wedding.

Elizabeth lets no grass grow under her feet. First, she calls the church secretary. Mrs. Kurtz confirms Saturday, December 19, at 4:30, for the wedding and Friday, December 18, at 5:30, to rehearse. Elizabeth looks at Mama who just overheard her two phone conversations. They clasp each other's hands and dance around the kitchen.

There is much to do in a short amount of time, but Elizabeth is energized. She pulls out her guest list for review, asking Mama what size wedding they have time to plan. Mama assures her, since this is a small town and it is easy to get things done without a lot of red tape, that she can have any size wedding she wants.

In addition, Mama reminds Elizabeth that they have friends who are experts in every area of weddings and receptions. She cautions Elizabeth, though, about spreading herself too thin, and encourages her to think through what is really important.

Getting married is really important to Elizabeth. The rest is fluff, but she wants to experience a lot of that fluff. Mama commits herself to making it work. The following Monday is reserved with Mindy, who bakes specialty cakes in her home. They make an appointment, for Tuesday with Ruby at the florist shop. On Thursday, Elizabeth, Mama, and Aunt Jan plan to drive to Nashville in search of the perfect, off-the-rack gown, since there is no time for ordering. Fortunately, Elizabeth is an exact size 8, and so should have a large selection from which to find her dream dress.

As Elizabeth finishes frying bacon and takes the biscuits from the oven, Mama reaches for the manila envelope on the phone desk, announcing more firmly than usual, "We must keep some sense of normalcy in our lives over these next several months."

Elizabeth is shocked, but someday she will understand that the changes affect Mama, too. She wants Elizabeth to move on with what is next in life; indeed, she is thrilled for her, but the wedding will be the end of an indescribably sweet era for Mama.

Their morning routine takes them past this uncomfortable moment. They finish breakfast and clean up the kitchen, then settle in for today's card, the last card, actually. It is from Aunt Jan.

"Sam, I have known you since you were in your mother's womb, and I watched you move those little arms and legs across her belly. You were a good boy, and you are now a kind man, but I have never expressed any of that to you in a meaningful way. The thing that stands out to me, and that I want to thank you specifically for, is providing wholesome summer fun for all the boys in Erwin. The boxes of baseballs, bats, and gloves that appear the first morning after school is out for the summer, every year at the vacant lot known simply as 'the field,' coincides exactly with your interest in every boy who plays.

"All the families of the ballplayers suspected you, but I realized the connection, for certain, the summer that I kept Phillip in Erwin, after his mother's life-threatening surgery. He came a week after the initial supplies were all claimed. Before I could purchase a glove for him, I saw you leave one, with a piece of paper attached, by the fence, in the early morning. Obviously, you expected no one else to be up and out, but I was. When I saw you, I did not know exactly what you were doing. But, later that day when Phillip came home from 'the field' for lunch, he had the glove and the paper with his name on it.

"Phillip uses that glove every summer when he returns to Erwin. You make a difference in boys learning teamwork. You personally made a difference to Phillip when you gave him that mysterious gift. It opened up a world of friendship in his part-time hometown. You did for him something that I could not do, and I am grateful."

Elizabeth's emotions are near the surface, with the long-awaited wedding now on the horizon, and with so much to do. Her eyes well up with tears, as she laments the fact that her father is not here to know this Phillip, in whom he invested so long ago, and who is about to be the husband of his little girl. Elizabeth thinks it is fitting that Mama chose Aunt Jan's letter about Phillip, as the last one to be read.

Mama calls Aunt Jan, and asks her if she remembers writing that letter. She says she surely does. She also still has the glove tucked away in its attic home, boxed with the piece of paper identifying it as Phillip's.

Aunt Jan, being the Type-A personality that she is, shows up at the back door within minutes holding a hastily dusted box, which they waste no time opening. Elizabeth holds the glove close, rubbing it and smelling it, as if it somehow brings her closer to her father. She examines the paper and realizes that she forms her upper case P's exactly like her father did, and she feels even more connected.

"Mama," she asks, "Who will walk me down the aisle, and give me away?"

"Well, Elizabeth," Mama replies, "In your childhood, I taught you much about the Savior. Later, you came back to me as a grown-up young lady who only needed guidance, but you have submitted to my leadership. I suppose that I am the one responsible for transferring your spiritual leadership from me to Phillip, since that is what a father who gives his daughter away to her husband at the wedding ceremony is about, transferring spiritual leadership. I will do it if you want me to, unless we come up with a better option."

In her heart, Mama wants a better option, but at the moment, one seems illusive to her.

## Chapter 39

At last, Sunday arrives and so does Phillip. He is pumped up over the job, and the fast-approaching wedding date. In the afternoon, he and Elizabeth decide to hike to their favorite spot in the woods by the stream, since it is a calm setting for getting their ducks in a row. They decide that Phillip's father should be his best man and that they will spend part of their honeymoon in Charleston with his mother.

Another thing that needs to be decided soon, for so many reasons, is the guest list. It will determine how many invitations to order, how much food they will need to have prepared for the reception, what size cake they need to order, and how many people from out of town will need accommodations. Phillip is going to pass the job of accommodations to Aunt Jan, whom he expects to be much more thorough than he would be. Besides, she is soliciting more involvement in this long-awaited event.

A big question for Phillip is whether he wants to be involved in the food selection, cake flavors, church decorations, and flowers, or if he prefers that to be the women's domain. Phillip says that he is fine being surprised by everything except the flowers. He wants to help decide on Elizabeth's bouquet. She is delighted with his response, since not having to run everything by him for approval can speed up the process and minimize the stresses of the time crunch. She is especially glad, though, that he chooses to be involved in the flowers, because, to him, they are a specific expression of his love.

Now she is rethinking her trip to Nashville for gown shopping, and considers driving to Atlanta, in hopes of having a bigger selection. Besides, she needs to talk to Suzette about being a bridesmaid. She could drive down on Thursday and stay through Sunday afternoon, then Phillip would not have to make the trip to Erwin, for a change.

On Sunday evening, Elizabeth phones Jeannie, Sue, and Stacy to ask them to be wedding attendants, and to get their sizes for the bridesmaid dresses.

Early on Monday, Elizabeth, Mama, and all the ladies go to check out cakes. The outing becomes their own special party, as they taste-test numerous flavors and look at pictures of other wedding receptions to help Elizabeth choose a style. Since she is most interested in something simple and traditional, the choice is easy.

All the ladies include themselves on the trip to the florist, where Elizabeth confirms the wedding date, studies pictures of bridesmaid bouquets, and makes an appointment for her and Phillip during his Thanksgiving break.

At this point, Elizabeth thinks that it all seems too easy. She wonders if this is an omen?

# Chapter 40

Arriving in Atlanta, Elizabeth knows she will get used to its vastness when she actually moves here; but for now, it seems overwhelming to her. She is at Suzette's church by 2:45, and helping her collate some booklets for a women's Bible study keeps Elizabeth occupied until Suzette's workday ends at 4:00. They head straight to the Phipps Plaza Mall, since it is open late and, as Suzette says, "We can cover many stores in a short amount of time."

An ideal outcome would be to find the bridal gown and the bridesmaid dresses in this one trip, preferably in one shop, and Elizabeth seeks a balance in her head between the likelihood and the hopefulness of that happening. There is a definite possibility with the bridesmaid dresses, since Elizabeth wants them to be festively and classically Christmas in design, and the stores are already carrying holiday clothing. Although Elizabeth has long groused about Christmas usurping Thanksgiving, that trend may work to her advantage this year.

The weekend is flying by with nonstop shopping, yielding a trunk full of goodies as Elizabeth shops alone on Friday, while

Phillip and Suzette work. She finds gifts for all her wedding party and for her special ladies. She also purchases a dress she considers just right for Mama, with the store's promise that it can be returned if it does not fit or is not to Mama's liking.

Though their trip from earlier in the week yielded no bridesmaid dresses, Saturday finds Suzette trying on dresses until she shouts, "No more!"

The two girls lean against the dressing room wall, slide to the floor exhausted, and laugh. They are happy to have narrowed the choice to a couple in the same store and decide to go home to soak their aching feet in a tub of hot water and take a nap.

Later, Phillip takes them to dinner at Applebee's, followed by more shopping. The girls declare it good practice for him, since he is about to become a married man. When Suzette models the first dress, a sleek, shimmering forest green with a flattering v-shaped neckline defined by a triple row of rhinestones that converge at the point with a teardrop, Phillip proclaims it his absolute personal favorite.

"Do you love it that much, or is that the quickest way you know to get this shopping trip over?" Elizabeth asks.

Phillip admits to teasing and says, "Bring on the next one."

When Suzette steps out of the dressing room, she is again striking in a black satin two-piece with a fuller pleated skirt that whispers femininity in the way it sways with each step. The fitted bodice is classic, with cap sleeves and a slight v-shape at the neckline and the waist. Its only embellishment is a line of simple rhinestone buttons down the front. Elizabeth finds it difficult to decide between the dresses, since she is drawn to them both, even though they are almost polar opposites, and each will give a vastly different look and feel to the wedding.

"It should be easy," she declares, as she thinks of her great appreciation for the fact that she has found two ideal choices during the first week of shopping. "But it is so very hard! " She is wishing for a way to decide, when the ridiculously obvious occurs to her. Check the availability of sizes. She finds that the black satin is available in each size, but the green is not.

"What a way to have that decision simplified," Elizabeth muses.

In thinking further, she sees that this dress will be much more flattering and easier for Jeannie and her prosthesis. She wonders why she did not think of that before, but she excuses herself, as her mind is going in a million directions. They purchase the dresses and Elizabeth takes them by the college, personally giving Jeannie and Stacey theirs to try on, and leaving Sue's with them for her to pick up on Monday. Jeannie's proves to be a perfect fit and Stacey's is slightly long, but Sue can easily alter it for her. The consensus is that they seem to be specifically designed for Elizabeth's wedding.

While driving home on Sunday afternoon, she relives the weekend and declares that although the time with Phillip was minimal, it was exceptional. She marvels at what has already been accomplished for the big day, but she is still waiting for the wedding dress of her dreams, which has never actually been defined in her dreams, but which she will know when she sees it.

Elizabeth arrives home at dusk to find Mama waiting in the swing, bundled in her double wedding ring quilt. As she pulls the car into the driveway, Mama flings off the quilt and meets Elizabeth at the car with open arms, for a hug, and for bags to carry in. It takes them each two trips to carry everything.

Elizabeth is anxious to show Mama her finds, so anxious that she wants to skip the potato soup Mama has simmering on the stove. But, she is hungry, so she rushes to eat. Then they are off to unpack.

As Elizabeth tucks the gifts away in her closet, she pronounces them off limits. She is glad that she brought Jeannie's dress with her to leave at Grandma's house. Now, she can show it to Mama instead of trying to describe it and feeling as if she failed to do it justice. Mama's face tells her all she needs to know, if she still had any doubt about this being the ideal dress.

Elizabeth hopes that since Mama is thrilled with the dresses for the girls, she will be as thrilled with her own. She mentally crosses her fingers as she lays it across the bed and carefully removes the plastic.

Mama looks at the tea-length, deep purple crepe dress, sprinkled liberally on the bodice with purple seed pearls. Its long-sleeved, matching jacket is trimmed in wide, monochromatic satin and fastens with a purple pearl clip. Mama stares at the dress for too long, hoping it belongs to her, but afraid to ask, which is out of character for a woman rarely afraid of anything.

"Try it on," Elizabeth encourages, breaking Mama's trance.

Mama makes quick work of changing and exclaims, "I have never looked so beautiful! A little shortening of the sleeves and this dress was made for me."

Soon after their morning routine, which no longer includes Sam's cards, Mama makes the one adjustment to her "grandmother of the bride" dress, so she can check another job off their growing list. She decides to leave her dress hanging on the outside of the closet door to admire repeatedly throughout the day.

Since the time is so short for ordering invitations, they are thankful for the closeness of a small town, and for the fact that etiquette here is what it was originally meant to be, manners and consideration. Mama says it will be fine to put the invitation in the church bulletin. For family and other friends, they will make phone calls.

"We're ahead of schedule," Elizabeth proclaims. "I think I will sleep in tomorrow." As she speaks, Elizabeth ignores a voice in her head warning her that being ahead of schedule rarely affords time to relax. Instead, it simply frees time for the next crisis.

## Chapter 41

She wakes the next morning to the sound of concern in Mama's voice as she speaks on the phone.

Who can she be talking to and why does her tone sound ominous, Elizabeth wonders, as she bounds down the hallway.

Mama tells her that Phillip is on the phone. Then, Aunt Jan arrives at the kitchen door and lets herself in. Elizabeth takes the phone, knowing something dreadful has happened.

"Phillip?" her trembling voice tells him to get right to the point without trying to soften the blow.

"My mother is gone," he says, stoically, like the good soldier he has been for a lifetime. But Elizabeth cannot even feign stoicism. Her emotional heart feels ripped away from his mother's too soon after they had so easily bonded in love for their Phillip and for each other. Sobs overtake her, shaking her lean frame to its core. She was one day, in an instant, tied in love to Mrs. Winn, and now that love can no longer express itself. She tries to understand God's purpose in taking Phillip's mother before the wedding and their planned honeymoon time with her. She tries, but understanding does not come. So she knows that trust, not understanding, is the operative attribute for now.

Elizabeth writes down Phillip's instructions.

Phillip says he wishes he could come to get her, but logistics demand that they meet in Charleston. He must turn in one more paper and take a quick test before he can be on his way, not needing to return until after Thanksgiving break.

Mama rushes out to Sam's for gas and a quick hose and belt check. Glenn brings her home with plans to return the car when it is ready. Meanwhile, Aunt Jan is packing and fixing breakfast for anyone who will eat.

When Mama chooses to drive, Elizabeth easily agrees. Navigating is second nature to Aunt Jan who has made this trip enough times to know everything about the way, except the latest road construction, which rears its ugly head about midway in the trip. But it is short-lived and the women are soon going full-speed ahead. It could have been a solemn trip, but Aunt Jan uses the time to add to Elizabeth's knowledge of her soon-to-be family. She pieces together fragments, comforting Elizabeth with the information.

Although Elizabeth's life once again seems privileged in many ways, she has suffered much loss in her short lifetime. It could be enough to devastate anyone, but she has, by virtue of her strength of character, risen above as she learns to find gratitude in all things. She is not grateful for the death of Mrs. Winn, but she is grateful in the midst of it, knowing it has eternal purpose.

Then she realizes that perhaps she is grateful for Phillip's mother's death, since it took her crippled body from this fallen world to glory.

Now crying for Mrs. Winn will bring only tears of joy. But

she cries tears of pain for Phillip and his father, and she cries them for herself.

Phillip has been worried about Elizabeth, but the instant he sees her from afar, he recognizes the calmness that has overtaken her spirit. And he is relieved.

The service is overflowing with people, which is no surprise. Mrs. Winn has been the town's heroine, in her own right, and by virtue of the fact that her husband has cherished her seemingly beyond human measure has made him the town's unsung hero. Town folks, who have respected the requests to not overwhelm Mrs. Winn with company, are now free to be open with their admiration.

Elizabeth is glad she has the wedding to occupy her mind, and she wonders if she is really on schedule as much as she once thought. She determines to escalate her efforts.

## Chapter 42

On Saturday, Phillip drives the ladies back to Erwin, arriving barely in time to get to the florist before closing time. He has Elizabeth pick out her bouquet from several pictures and discreetly makes arrangements with Deborah to call about a sentimental addition. Together, they choose the flowers for the bridesmaids and maid of honor. Nosegays of red roses with babies breath and fern, they agree, will add the precise amount of festivity to the classic black dresses.

Since Phillip had flown to Charleston and driven with the ladies to Erwin, Elizabeth decides to drive Phillip back to Emory on Monday. Besides, she needs another trip to Atlanta to continue her search for that perfect wedding dress. She is beginning to panic over not having found it yet. The wedding is less than a month away, and sometimes she wonders if they should have given themselves more time. It is hard to put a wedding together in three months, even a simple one in Erwin.

The trip to Atlanta yields great visiting time with Phillip on the ride down, and an unusually fun time with Suzette, who has borrowed chick flick videos from a friend for a marathon evening of laughing, crying, and chocolate eating.

The trip, however, does not yield a wedding dress. However, her panic subsides, and she cannot explain that, except that the situation now seems funny rather than frustrating. She keeps envisioning herself walking down the aisle in one of the bridesmaid dresses, and the headline above the wedding picture in the local newspaper reads: "Where's the bride?????"

She and Mama head to Nashville on Tuesday to search the shops there. The results are the same as in Atlanta. They discuss their options on the ride home and come up with nothing. After turning into their driveway, they notice a UPS truck stopping in front of the house.

Elizabeth quips, "He is here to deliver me the perfect wedding dress."

She and Mama laugh as Mama says, "I wish."

The box from Phillip's father is surprisingly light for its size. Mama and Elizabeth expect it is a wedding present. Elizabeth rips into it with anticipation. Inside, she finds the present wrapped in multiple layers of white tissue paper with a handwritten note taped to the top. Mama moves closer as Elizabeth reads the note from Mr. Winn.

"Elizabeth, as I was going through Fran's things today for closure, I held this dress in my arms as I replayed every moment of our wedding in my mind. I am sure that a girl, a woman, as sensitive as you, and who instantly loved Fran as if you had been born to love her..." Elizabeth chokes up and can no longer read aloud.

Mama takes over without missing a breath, "...would like

this as a remembrance of your unique bond. I know, in my heart, that you will cherish it.

Much love,

Dad"

Elizabeth's trembling fingers gently unfold the tissues to reveal chiffon over satin. Full inspection shows an ever so slightly scooped neckline and an empire waist defined with a white satin band that ties into an embellished bow in back. The skirt has a slight flair with a small sewn-in crinoline for body, and the sleeves are capped much like those of the bridesmaid dresses.

Mama and Elizabeth look at each other, thinking the same thought, and rush toward Mama's bedroom, as it is closest. The moment Elizabeth slips into this vintage wonder, she knows it is hers in more ways than one. It needs nothing except cleaning and pressing from the years of being in storage.

"Of course, I could not find the perfect wedding dress in the shops of Georgia and Tennessee, since it was waiting for me in a closet in South Carolina," Elizabeth tells Mama.

The very next day, they are in Nashville to again peruse the bridal shops, with a new focus. Today, they are looking for precisely the right veil to go with the perfect dress. The consultant finds it immediately, after seeing the dress and hearing the story. She chooses a short bouffant veil attached to a small satin band. Elizabeth and Mama agree that it compliments the dress and fulfills the vintage look.

Aunt Jan asks Elizabeth to model it all for her, and she knows instantly what she will suggest that Phillip get Elizabeth for a wedding gift.

Elizabeth calls Phillip to tell him that she has found a dress, which he asks her to describe to him.

Playfully she responds, "And spoil the surprise?"

# Chapter 43

Phillip finishes his last exam and hops in the car, which is already packed and facing north for a quick getaway. Arriving late, he finds everyone waiting up for him. Mama and Aunt Jan are glad to see him safely home, giving him a warm hug before leaving him with his Elizabeth.

The next morning, Phillip wakes up before Aunt Jan has breakfast ready, and announces that he will serve her.

As they rush to fill each other in on their separate worlds, Aunt Jan asks, "Do you have Elizabeth's wedding gift yet? Because, if you don't, I know exactly what you should get her."

Phillip looks amusingly shocked, as Aunt Jan is rarely one to offer an opinion.

"Go on," he encourages her.

"I have seen her dress and I think it is begging for a strand of pearls. Now she could buy them herself or one of us ladies could give them to her. However, since pearls are described in the Scriptures as having great value, and they are a favorite wedding gem because of their high association with love, it would be much more appropriate and tender if they came from you. It just seems to me that pearls from you would be extremely thoughtful."

Phillip likes the suggestion. Another idea springs out of this information and adds itself to the mental list of surprises he has planned for Elizabeth's future.

During the week, Elizabeth enjoys one more shower, which fulfills her needs for setting up a well-stocked kitchen. In addition, she has a luncheon at Mrs. Sim's for the girls in the wedding party. It is a happy time filled with giggles and wonder and sweet innocence.

Time is passing too quickly to get things done in leisurely manner, but not quickly enough for the bride and groom. Thursday arrives with last-minute errands, one of which Elizabeth almost allows to get lost in the shuffle. She could put it off until after the wedding, but she does not want to. She calls Phillip to join her at 10:00, to squeeze in a short trip to the service station. Elizabeth has completed her paperwork with the help of Mama, her lawyer, and the bank. And she has her speech prepared, but she has also written it in a letter, both for posterity and in case she chokes up with sentiment.

Mama is included, to tape the presentation with her video camera and to support Elizabeth in what Mama calls a generous decision. But to Elizabeth, it is an act of gratitude. Bob and Glenn are busy, but Billy senses something, and comes in from changing a battery to take over the register.

They all crowd into the tiny office, where Elizabeth takes Bob and Glenn each by the hand and says, with a strong voice, "You were Daddy's friends till his death, and you have been my friends, faithfully and honestly providing for me the way Daddy arranged for you to do. This weekend, you will witness me marrying a wonderful man who is fully capable of providing for me."

She slides her hands free to pass them the legal-sized envelope that Phillip has been guarding for her, and says, "This envelope contains all the paperwork to make Sam's Service Station yours, effective in two weeks, on January 1. All that is required is your notarized signatures in the presence of Mama's lawyer. It is my gift to you."

She is amazed at having made her speech without tears. However, she is watching two grown men cry. Bob is first to reach for her. He picks her up and bear-hugs her, the way he used to when she was eight. He knows that today is not a day for those reserved hugs Elizabeth has been getting from him since returning to Erwin as an adult. Glenn, one to be calmer in his approach, kisses her forehead and wipes his eyes again with his shirtsleeve.

Saying "thank you" just doesn't seem like enough to the men, but Elizabeth assures them that it is enough for her.

Elizabeth and Phillip spend Thursday evening with Morgan and Jeannie and as many friends as can drop by. Mama serves wassail and cookies, and they sing carols around the piano. The house is full of pianists, so they take turns providing a concert of different styles. Elizabeth's preference is Stacey, as her touch is gentle, so much like her personality.

By the end of the evening, the women have gravitated to the kitchen and are sitting around the table, while the men are hanging out by the fireplace discussing football.

Phillip takes Morgan with him to the Nashville airport to pick up his father at midnight. The ride is a great time for some serious man-to-man talking. Morgan confides in Phillip that he has been in love with Jeannie since early on, but would not let himself acknowledge it until he saw her on his turf. Life in Australia is not like life in America, he says, and not many girls would or could easily adjust.

"But while she was there," Morgan adds, "it became clear to me that it is not where you live or how different the customs are, it is that you serve the same Lord and you have the same family values. The bonus, which I have relished since our first meeting but had not previously factored into this equation, is Jeannie's adaptable spirit."

There is a long pause and then he continues, "I am chomping at the bit to be open about my deepest feelings to her and to give her a ring, but a wedding would be so far off. He sighs, then adds with intense feeling, "It is hard," as if he is the only one to ever experience such a thing.

Phillip smiles a knowing smile and pats Morgan on the shoulder, the way men do.

Phillip spends Friday morning driving his father around the little town that he once knew so well but now finds to be an enigma of two time periods trying to co-exist, and seemingly succeeding. He remembers the old Erwin and enjoys it, especially when they ride out to Jimmy's and find it virtually unchanged from three decades ago. Will and Jimmy embrace and reminisce. Will promises to visit more now. He needs diversions, as it is not only the loneliness of his heart, but also the emptiness of his schedule that looms over him like a specter. He needs to make plans that keep him busy.

Phillip had once viewed his parents' relationship as a one-way street, because that was all his young mind could comprehend. Now there is a new view. His father was not only dutiful, but also enamored, with a loving wife who could seemingly return so little. But for his father, it was enough.

Phillip's father asks his sister, Aunt Jan, for something to do, and she gives him recipes to put in order in her file box. While filing them alphabetically by categories, he runs across some of his childhood favorites, and searches the stack for empty note cards to copy them for Elizabeth. On the bottom of each, he draws a smiley face to remind her each time she prepares it, that it will make someone happy.

The rehearsal runs smoothly, and they arrive early for dinner in the fellowship hall, to enjoy h'ors d'oeuvres and piano music as they wait for everyone to settle in.

Several ladies of the church have prepared a four-course meal that is conducive to the roasting and toasting of the bride and groom.

The best man, Phillip's father, begins with a toast to the couple, charging them to love, above all. He shares his own wedding day memories and how it actually took his breath away when he saw Fran enter through the double doors of the church sanctuary on her father's arm, wearing a celestial dress and a wispy veil that shadowed her face but did not dim her radiance.

"Phillip, I wish for you a similar vision of loveliness to carry with you all your days," he says

Elizabeth's mentoring ladies put on a skit about cooking failures and how they can be overcome by a loving husband who calls for takeout. Her college girlfriends commit to be as diligent as ever to continuing their friendship and accountability with each other concerning their walk with the Lord. After their serious part is over, they read husband jokes about football widows and which one has the most new clothes in her closet from shopping on game days.

To the bridal attendants, Elizabeth presents quartz earrings to wear in the wedding and journals for the new year. Once a month, Elizabeth will begin a round-robin email with an event out of the journal to share with all the others. "It will be part of our accountability and our way of staying current in each one's everyday happenings," she tells them.

Phillip lifts his glass to toast the two women who have been instrumental in pointing two children, Elizabeth and himself, to the Lord; two children, as Phillip says, who would grow up to embrace Him personally and plan a life of serving Him together.

Finally, Phillip and Elizabeth exchange wedding gifts. She gives him a computer program of the Bible and one of Strong's Concordance to make it easier for him to be the strong leader he has committed to her that he will be. These are accompanied by a card that says it all: "You are mine, I am yours, and we are His."

Phillip then takes the string of pearls from it's satin box, holds it in the light, and explains that this is the only gem that needs no cutting or shaping to show its beauty. He lays it in her open hands and says, "Elizabeth, these pearls represent high value. They are associated with love and beauty, both of which characterize you. They are yours to wear for the first time tomorrow with your wedding dress and ever after, as a symbol of your great value to me."

The party has gone on longer than expected, and there is little time to sleep before the scurry of the wedding day. Although Elizabeth's body screams for rest, her mind is filled with details of tomorrow's schedule, and her heart is filled with incredible excitement.

# Chapter 44

Elizabeth slips into Mama's room before the sun comes up and slides under the covers beside her, reaching for her hand to give it three little squeezes, meaning "I love you," the way she used to do when she was a little girl. She wants to savor this last morning with Mama before their situation changes to what is next and what is right, but what is also somewhat like tearing her heart out. She knows that Mama probably feels it more keenly than she does, though she can't imagine how. This is her gift to Mama, a treasured and tender display of her gratitude and love.

Mama looks at Elizabeth and smiles, then reaches over to smooth her tousled hair behind her ear, reminiscent of those childhood times when she wanted to see Elizabeth's face.

"Mama," Elizabeth says, "The memory of your warmth will comfort me when we are apart. I will bring honor to you for all my days."

On Mama's dresser, Elizabeth has laid a small crosstitch for Mama to find later that reads, "'She openeth her mouth with wisdom; and in her tongue is the law of kindness.' Proverbs 31:26"

Mama tells Elizabeth not to move, while she goes to her

closet and takes out the box. Elizabeth is puzzled as she thinks they have read every letter and card. She thinks that perhaps Mama is giving her the box for her very own. She sits up and watches as Mama takes out an aged, but not worn, manila envelope. It is then that Elizabeth flashes back to the day that Mama first opened her father's box and removed several thin envelopes, putting them in her closet to await their appropriate time.

Mama brings Elizabeth back to the present when she presents this envelope face up to Elizabeth so that she sees the familiar handwriting of her father, the familiar shaky handwriting matching Phillip's letter. But this one is to her and says, "To My Grown-up Elizabeth on Her Wedding Day." Elizabeth's hands tremble and her lips quiver. Her eyes are too full for clear vision, so she simply holds the envelope to her chest.

Mama bends to kiss her cheek before asking if Elizabeth wants privacy to read this letter.

"Yes, I do," she replies, with a catch in her voice.

It is a long letter, most of which was dictated to her mother, who recorded it word for word. It generally recounts her almost nine years with him, and the joy she brought to his life. It includes details of each holiday, and every birthday. Many of the things, Elizabeth does not remember; some, she remembers vaguely; and others she remembers vividly, thinking it uncanny that her responses to the memories are so much like the responses her father relates. Near the end, the handwriting becomes his again.

"Elizabeth," she reads, "on this day of your marriage, I cannot walk you down the aisle, but I have done it so many times in my mind during these months of illness. I tried to picture you and think that I came close. As a child, while I am writing this, you look so much like your truly beautiful mother, so that is how I think you must look today as you read this. If I could be there, I would stand tall with my chest puffed out at the thrill of walking you down the aisle to give you away to the man of your dreams. He is, I feel certain, the man of my dreams, also, since you will have picked him under the guidance of the Lord. I would lift your veil and kiss your cheek, dropping a tear of joy at your happiness. When asked, 'Who gives this woman to be married to this man?' I would answer with resolve, 'I do,' knowing that it is my privileged job and mine alone. I am asking, when that time comes, for you to play the tape that is safely waiting in another envelope that Mama has for you. It has several renditions of me saying, 'I do.' You have what you need to make me able to give you away in the presence of your wedding guests, on this your wedding day, and during your wedding ceremony.

I love you!

Daddy"

Elizabeth flies into the kitchen to show the letter to Mama and ask for the other envelope. Mama's eyes are moist with forming tears as she begins reading, but the tears flood her face and drip off her chin as she gets to the part about Sam's tape recording. It is the answer to her quandary.

She wipes her face repeatedly with her apron, composes herself, and goes to her closet again to retrieve yet another manila envelope. This one also says, "To My Grown-up Elizabeth on Her Wedding Day." In the corner is a small #2 with a note that says, "Not to be opened until after #1 has been read." Elizabeth looks back at the other envelope and notices for the first time that it has a small #1 in its corner.

Popping the tape into the recorder on the telephone desk, Elizabeth listens intently with Mama, as her father recites the words, "I do," at least a dozen times with different inflections and degrees of loudness and softness. The crying is over for this moment. Now, they can only smile.

Elizabeth and Mama decide that she will walk down the short aisle alone, while Mama fills the role that is truly hers, grandmother of the bride.

# Chapter 45

Elizabeth chooses to change in the church choir room with the other girls, where they see her dress and hear its story for the first time. Elizabeth loves sharing the surprise of the dress. Her bridesmaids attend to her well, putting on her pearls, pinning the veil securely in place, and even slipping on her shoes so she will not wrinkle her dress. The florist brings in all the flowers and Elizabeth sees her bouquet for the first time since picking it out from a picture. Its fully opened white roses, mingled with white buds and babies breath, are set off by trailing green fern and ivy. It is even lovelier than she remembered.

Phillip asked permission from the beginning to have input in the flowers. Because he knew she wanted it to be white for the pictures, he had two intertwined removable red roses attached to the back, as a symbol of the two becoming one. She decides not to remove them.

When Mama is escorted down the aisle to her privileged seat as grandmother of the bride, there is a slight buzz among the congregation as to who will walk Elizabeth down the aisle and give her away. Many had expected Mama to fill that role.

The girls are lined up in the foyer as the organ music plays. Through a little crack in the doorway, Elizabeth can see Phillip and his men enter, but he cannot see her. He doesn't look nervous. And she wonders if perhaps she is nervous enough for them both.

Each bridesmaid comes down the aisle and takes her place on the steps mere seconds before the bridal march begins. Then two ushers open the double doors for Elizabeth to enter. Phillip recognizes the dress from his parent's wedding picture, which hangs above the piano in his father's living room. His mind flashes back to his father's wish for him last night that he would have a similar vision of loveliness to carry with him for all his days. He drinks in the total picture, savoring detail after detail, committing it all to his memory. Then, he focuses only on Elizabeth's face and their eyes lock momentarily before he follows her gaze to his father, whose smile confirms that he is surprised and ever so pleased.

As Elizabeth takes her place before the pastor and beside her soon-to-be husband, she breathes a small sigh of contentment at her nearly secret plan.

The quiet buzz continues, as people turn to sit back down, puzzled that no one walked Elizabeth down the aisle and still wondering who will give her away.

When the pastor addresses the bride and groom about the meaning of marriage and the meaning of being given away by the father to the leadership and protection of the husband, the congregational confusion escalates. Truly, this turn of events is even baffling to Phillip and the entire bridal party, since that is not how they practiced it the day before.

Soon the pastor comes to the much-awaited question, "Who gives this woman to be married to this man?" A deep silence falls over the auditorium, which sets the stage perfectly for the kind voice of Elizabeth's father coming from a recorder hidden among the flowers, pronouncing a reverberating, "I do."

Unknown to Elizabeth, this consent is followed by another message that her father had prepared for the pastor who would perform the ceremony, an explanation from her father's faltering, but determined voice.

"Though I will not be there for your wedding, as I will not be there to watch you grow up, I have total confidence that you will grow sweetly and in grace and will choose the ideal man for your husband, so I am blessing your wedding day and your marriage in advance while I have the breath to do so. You will receive this blessing at the proper time and with the understanding that only the Lord's plan for me to be home with Him preempts my doing this in person and by your side. I love you, my precious Elizabeth."

The solemnity of the service is brought totally back into focus. The ceremony continues through the music and vows with hardly a dry eye among the guests, and certainly not between the bride and groom. Upon their being pronounced man and wife, Phillip kisses his bride and whispers in her ear, "How did you pull that one off?"

Smiles and quiet chatter are abundant as the recessional music follows the wedding party outside, down the winding path, and to the reception in the rose atrium. Meanwhile Phillip and Elizabeth sneak a quick detour into Pastor Mitchell's study for a private moment that affords them a long look into each other's faces, a more intimate kiss, and an embrace that magnifies their matching heartbeats, reminding Elizabeth that her life is a series of finding herself blessed.

The End

# Need additional copies?

To order more copies of *Finding Herself Blessed*, contact NewBookPublishing.com

- ❐ Order online at NewBookPublishing.com
- ❐ Call 877-311-5100 or
- ❐ Email Info@NewBookPublishing.com

*Call for multiple copy discounts!*

Author's email
JanieUpchurch@mac.com

Author's website
www.JanieUpchurch.com

Reliance Media